The Rules

D. J. Kirkby

e-book and paperback editions published by
Sunnyside Press
Cover design by DesignforWriters.com
Story Copyright © D.J. Kirkby 2015
First Edition
Dee Kirkby asserts the moral right under the Copyright, Designs and Patents Act 1988 to be identified as the author of this work.
All Rights reserved. No part of this publication may be reproduced, stored in a retrieval system or transmitted, in any form or by any means without the prior consent of the author, nor be otherwise circulated in any form of binding or cover other than that which it is published and without a similar condition being imposed on the subsequent purchaser.

ISBN: 0957557752
ISBN-13: 978-0-9575577-5-8

Author Website: D.J.Kirkby: djkirkby.co.uk

The Rules

D. J. Kirkby

For my mum who will say Cody is rascal
and
for my husband, son and stepsons
I love you all up

Prequel - The Maverick

'There he is!' Cody spotted the tatty cat climbing over the fence in the garden and rushed out to make a fuss of him with his sisters following close behind, slamming the door in their excitement.

'I think it's really mean of you to name him after some old boxer.'

'Mean? That's all you know. Joey DeJohn was a legend! Even if he did have a scrunched up face.'

Sandy and Lizzie secretly thought him too sweet to be named after a sportsman and agreed with each other that 'Marmalade' suited him better. They didn't want to complain though, for they knew that if they didn't go along with Cody's choice he would be grumpy and impatient with them until they agreed with his choice of name. The girls knew how to keep the peace; they'd watched their mother defer to their father for years now. Each day the children snuck food from their meagre portions to feed to Joey. Cody and his sisters would crowd happily round Joey, marvelling that he managed to purr as he ate. During meals he would allow them to smooth his fur, arching his back against their passing hands. Their back yard was little more than concrete and coarse grass but these discomforts blurred during these stolen moments in time, gifting them with the illusion that their world was a calm and peaceful place. A reality filled with the soothing sensations that were a by-product of stroking a warm, purring, *although distinctly smelly*, giver of comfort.

While Cody's mother occasionally encouraged these stolen moments with Joey, the children knew their father most certainly would not. No childhood magic for Edward's brood *thankyouverymuch*! He believed that the sooner they faced the harsh realities of life, the better prepared they would be. That very day he caught them enjoying their unacceptable moments of cat magic when he came home early from work. There had been a fire at the factory and it was now closed until the damage could be repaired. The 'fwhick' of the gate latch disengaging from the catch penetrated their happy haze too slowly for them to be able to shoo Joey away. They looked at each other in horror knowing that only their father used the back gate. Why had he come home early? They knew that the very act of feeding Joey, when their father wasn't supposed to be home, would convince him that they were being deliberately deceitful. Guilt blushed across their faces because rule one was: never lie and rule two was: waste not, want not. As one they turned and, too scared to look at his face, they instead watched his boots make contact with the concrete, each loud step bringing him closer to Joey.

Despite their pathetic attempts to shield him, Edward could see the mangy cat licking the pavement. No work equalled no money, and the sight of them feeding a stray incensed him beyond reason. He reached between the girls, easily parting their joined hands. He took a half step then followed through with his other leg. The toe of his boot connected with Joey's body, transferring enough momentum to send him flying over the fence. The children heard Joey squeal once. Then painfully weighted silence descended on both sides of the fence. As one, they turned toward their father, hollow with the knowledge that they would be next to feel the impact of his wrath.

He glared at them and then words poured from his mouth, riding the crest of his anger. 'Stealing food and feeding it to a stray? You don't have a clue do 'ya? Not a clue.'

They flinched, nodded and then hastily shook their heads... confused.

Edward's face darkened. 'Food costs money, something which you contribute none of. Rule one and rule two – broken at the same time! I don't work my ass off so that you can feed perfectly good food to mangy strays and try to lie about it when I catch you!'

Snatching up the remains of the fish, he grabbed Cody's chin firmly, tilting it up until Cody was forced to look him in the eye. 'Don't be a loser all your life!'

Rule three sharpened with his father's harsh tone sliced though Cody as he watched his dad kick aside a sun-bleached plastic ball and stomped into the house.

Guiltily relieved at their escape, the children tuned out the sound of their father's voice shouting at their mother and loitered outside whispering Joey's name, hoping for a meow in response, until their mother called them for supper. Cody and his sisters slunk in.

The children were too scared by what Joey's continued silence might mean to give much thought to the fact that they remained unpunished. After quickly washing their hands, they sat on the wooden bench between the chilly outside facing wall and table. Their father was po-faced at the head of the table, making eye contact only with the television that sat precariously on a narrow shelf above their mother's chair. Betty served them their meal, lips pressed into a thin line, her face as pale and bleak as the soup she put before them. Cody and his sisters looked down at their bowls and realised with horror that this was their punishment; the fish scales floated iridescently on top of the thin milky broth. Edward slurped his soup loudly. The rest of the family quietly tried to swallow without the food touching their tongue.

Cody kept his gaze on the table for fear his rage would be visible in his eyes. The view of the scarred and pitted beige surface did little to calm him. He wondered why the heat of his angry stare didn't burn holes in the table.

Cody flinched when the phone rang in the next room and again when his father heaved himself out of the chair to go answer it. Cody grabbed the tin of sewing machine oil that sat on the window ledge behind him and squirted, then stirred some into his father's soup bowl. The thin walls were no barrier to the peaks and troughs of the angry sounding mutters that emanated from their father's side of the phone conversation in the next room. Oddly, the silence that followed the phone making contact with its cradle was no less disturbing than the noise that had preceded it. When their father returned to the table, they were all innocently stirring their soup.

Cody dared not look at his sisters when their father picked up his spoon. He could feel them trembling on either side of him as they fought to suppress the urge to giggle hysterically. The sharp edge of their mother's palpable fear quickly rendered them poker faced. Their father cast a suspicious glare over them before spooning the remainder of his soup into his mouth with his eyes fixed unwaveringly on the television for the rest of the meal.

~ ~

The repeated sound of his father's footfall on the landing between the toilet and bedroom that night gave Cody a funny swoopy feeling in his stomach; the kind he got when he was a little bit scared and a little bit happy. To stop himself from feeling bad for feeling happy with the result of his rebellion against his father's rules, he pulled his dictionary out from under his blanket. Turning to the correct page in the M section he once again read the reassuring definition for maverick:

Someone who refuses to play by the rules and exhibits great independence in thought and action

Cody the Maverick made sure the book couldn't be seen in its hiding place under his bed before he fell asleep.

Chapter one – Cordbridge

'Awww crap!' Cody's voice came out as a pinched squeal after the hammer slipped and smashed onto his thumb. Fighting back tears and the sick feeling in his gut, and too scared to inspect the damage himself, he forced himself to lift his arm up as a signal to the first aider that he needed help. He could feel something trickling down his arm and cast a swift glance at the workhorse, and the sawdust covered ground below, looking for any bits of thumb that might have been sheared off by the force of the hammer blow.

'What 'choo gone 'n done boy?' Scary Harry said in his giant's voice that belied his small frame.

'Slipped. With hammer. Stripping frames.' Cody spoke through his teeth in an attempt to control the tremble in his voice.

Scary Harry took Cody's hand in his and examined it. 'Needs cleaning.'

'Will that hurt?'

'Not overly much.'

Cody kept his gaze averted and tried not to pass out from the pain as Scary Harry busied himself doing antiseptic smelling things to his thumb.

'You could do with a stitch or two.'

'As if it doesn't hurt enough already? No chance! Just wrap it tight, that'll do.'

'It'll take longer to heal, leave a big scar.'

Scary Harry's threat did nothing to change Cody's mind. 'I'll take my chances.'

Scary Harry shook his head and muttered ominously as he strapped Cody's thumb with a plaster before stomping off in the direction of the foreman.

Cody tried to decipher the look on the foreman's face as he listened to Scary Harry who gesticulated frequently during the short monologue.

Always someone got to try and interfere... as if I'm not a grown man who knows his own mind. Cody could feel his shoulders lift defensively as the foreman walked towards him.

'Lissen Tuttle, the deal is this, you get that thumb seen to properly, stitches are in order I'm led to believe, and then you kin have the rest of the day off with pay.'

'I don't need 'em Mike... can carry on as I am.' Cody tried not to wince as he grabbed hold of the frame with his sore hand.

'You've bled through that already.' The foreman pointed at the plaster on Cody's thumb. 'I'm not having you bleeding all over the place for the rest of the afternoon. If you won't see sense and get some stitches put in it then you'll have to take the day off unpaid. I'll see you back here Monday with or without stitches and will sort your pay then. Your choice.'

Cody walked home slowly. The new plaster that Scary Harry had put on felt too tight and he looked around trying to distract himself from the throb in his thumb. The sawmill was surrounded by a housing estate that had grown up around the site in the past few years. The city of Cordbridge was built in a series of squares which radiated out from the city hall and police headquarters in the centre, giving way to the large housing estate, small airport, steel works and shopping mall at each corner. Cody had always felt hemmed in by the town with its perfect squares of building lined streets, which allowed him no option to wander off in a random direction that didn't involve a straight road.

A man needs room to roam he thought in disgust, the yearning for a different way of life growing within him almost to bursting point. *One of these days I'm going to get away from this city life.*

Cody slouched in through his parents' front door and went upstairs to look for a plaster in the bathroom. Blood had soaked through the one on his thumb again.

'Hi Cody, you're home early.' His mum's voice sounded tight.

'Hurt myself.' Cody replied, half wondering why his mum sounded different, half wondering how to best place the inadequate plaster over the cut in order to stem the blood that kept oozing out.

His mother poked her head out of her bedroom with an anxious look on her face. 'Where? How?' she began, and then saw his finger. 'Oh...'

'It's not too bad mum, just won't stop bleeding.'

'Well... get some ice from the freezer, wrap it in a towel and press that on your finger, that'll help.'

Cody went and did as his mum had suggested, getting blood on the ice tray as he tried and failed to twist it to snap out the cubes without using his thumb. He pressed the towel against his thumb wondering what his mum was doing in her bedroom that had her so preoccupied that it meant she didn't offer to make the ice pack for him. It wasn't until he sat on her bed, hand cradled between his thigh and ice pack that he realised she was packing a suitcase.

'What you doing mum? I didn't know you and dad were going away.'

'We're not, uh, I am.'

'On your own? Where?' Cody's voice rose on a surge of surprise.

'A weekend quilting workshop. Time to make a start on keeping us warm this winter,' she said before twitching the edges of her mouth into a small smile. She lifted the clothes already in the suitcase to show him the partially made quilt neatly folded on the bottom alongside a stack of quilting squares waiting to be added.

Women's stuff. Cody's curiosity immediately morphed into boredom. 'Right. Well. Great. Have fun.' He stood to leave, ice pack dangling from his good hand. Unprepared for his mum's fierce hug which caught his left arm under hers, he returned her affection by patting her back gently with his sore hand. 'I'm going to lie down for a bit, rest up till supper time.'

'I've left a stew in the slow cooker. Should last you and your dad a couple of days. Bye son.' She cleared her throat and went back to flinging things in her suitcase.

Cody wondered if he was imagining that his mum was behaving a bit oddly but this fleeting awareness was soon overridden by his urge to get to sleep in the hopes that his finger would hurt less when he woke.

~~

'Joan?' His father's bellow woke Cody from a deep sleep. He bolted upright, heart pounding frantically for a few seconds before realising from the shadows in his room and the fact that his dad was home meant that it must be almost suppertime. He lay still for a moment, coming to terms with being awake, waiting for his heart to slow down to a normal pace. He heard his father curse and the squeak of the springs in his father's favourite chair told him he'd sat down to unlace and remove his work boots. Cody sat up and placed his feet on the floor, scrubbing his face with his hands, being careful not to put any pressure on his cut thumb. He examined it; glad to see the bleeding had stopped, happy that although it was still throbbing, it hurt less than it had earlier. He took a deep breath and made his way out of his room.

'Joan? What you up to woman?' His dad yelled, louder this time, as he heard Cody's movements upstairs.

'No dad, it's me.'

'Oh. Well where the hell's your mum got to then?'

Cody was already half way into the bathroom when his father asked this question and waited until he was downstairs before he responded.

'I saw her packing earlier. Guess she's already left.' He tested the kettle to see how full it was before flicking it on.

'Eh?' His father looked at him with an incredulous expression.

'Her quilting thing, she said she was going away to something to do with quilting, she'd packed that new one she started, the pink one.' Cody held up a mug in his father's direction, followed it with a questioning look.

His father nodded. 'Oh, yup. She asked a while back if she could go, said she had some pin money saved, said she'd see we were sorted for meals. I didn't think that was this weekend though...' his father trailed off and lifted the lid on the slow cooker. 'N'uff in here for a couple a days all right. So, I'll drink my tea, get washed up while you set the table and then we'll eat.' Edward sunk his weary 54-year-old bones into his chair, shook an unfiltered cigarette from its pack, flicked his lighter into flame and waited for Cody to bring him his mug.

A please would be nice, Cody thought to himself and wondered yet again how his mother managed to put up with his father all these years.

Chapter two - Grown up and gone away

Cody brought his dad a mug of tea and went back into the kitchen to set the table for supper. The painkillers he had taken before making the ice pack had worn off and his finger had gone from throbbing persistently to blaring pain waves again. Cody took another two painkillers from the cupboard above the stove. He looked at the list his oldest sister Sandy had taped to the inside of the cupboard; it was beginning to yellow with age now. The list had been part of a chemistry project she had done when she was still in high school and it detailed how often they could take each medicine and what one was best for which ailment. Cody smiled. Sandy was organised to the extreme and always had been; right from birth his mum said. Cody's parents were married the year Sandy was born and she had turned twenty-six last month. How does a marriage like mum and dad's survive twenty-six years? Cody wondered. Both of his sisters had used marriage as a vehicle to get them out of the tyranny that ruled life in their parental home, though Cody wasn't convinced that they had found greener pastures in their own marriages.

Sandy's husband, George was a private in the army and spent most of his time grousing about the fact that Canada had refused to get involved in various conflicts around the world, and Cody had seen Sandy suffering the verbal brunt of his frustration. Cody thought George was just plain nuts, both for enlisting in the first place and for actually wanting to go and fight. Even worse,

George was an *angry* nutter whom Cody thought was as dangerous as wet dynamite with a slow burning fuse. Cody kept his opinion to himself however; he had seen enough anger in his short life to know that all he wanted to do was avoid confrontations. *If Sandy wants to let George treat her like dad treats mum then who am I to interfere?* Cody would think when feelings of guilt for not defending his sister crept under his emotional guard. Nowadays, Cody's father pretty much left him alone if he made himself inconspicuous enough, and Cody liked that so much more than the alternative. His father only seemed to have two moods as far as Cody could tell; sullen or shouting.

Lizzie's husband Charles, on the other hand, seemed neither sullen nor shouty. He was much older than her, thirty-seven years old when he married twenty-three year old Lizzie last year. Although kind and lovingly gentle with his wife, Charles was as demanding of Lizzie's time and attention as a young child. Cody's father said there was something perverse about a man who would marry a woman almost young enough to be his child and refused to acknowledge Charles's presence. At family gatherings Edward would speak to Lizzie only if forced to do so and then in nothing more than a monotone as he had not yet forgiven her for defying him by marrying Charles, despite Edward making it very clear to Lizzie that he disapproved of her choice of husband. Charles would stoically endure these experiences, standing with his arm protectively around Lizzie or clutching her hand as he followed her from room to room, ensuring they made an early escape to the comfort of their own home. Although Cody thought Charles was a bit wet for a man of his age, he had to admit that he fit the stereotype of an accountant very well and his personality seemed to be a good match for Lizzie. She had spent most of their childhood trying to mother anything that stood still long enough and seemed content to do the same for her husband. Not for the first time, Cody wondered how she would cope when she had a real baby of her own who would undoubtedly interfere with Charles's demands for her undivided attention. He suspected Lizzie wouldn't be quite so content then but for now, at least, she seemed blissfully unaware that her husband's behaviour was obviously immature.

Edward banged his mug down on the sideboard, bringing Cody back to the present with a start. 'You gonna stand in a daze all evening boy? I'll be wanting my supper when I come back down in five minutes, so you'd best get that table set 'n all.'

Cody shut the cupboard, took a deep breath to clear his head and said, 'I'll get on with it as soon as I've taken these tablets dad.'

'What'cha need tablets for?' his father asked grumpily.

Cody held up his sore hand.

'You done it at work? You wash it in antiseptic?'

Cody nodded. 'First aider did. Hurt like buggery.'

'You should try being grateful for his help instead of complaining.' Edward called out as he climbed the stairs.

'You should try acting like less of a prick.' Cody muttered quietly once he was certain his father was out of earshot. He swallowed the tablets dry, wincing at the bitter taste and he busied himself with placing crockery and cutlery on the table with more force than necessary.

Chapter three - Thin gold band

The weekend passed slowly. Edward had demanded Cody's help all day Saturday and true to form, they spent the day together in virtual silence. Cody's finger was throbbing by the time they had finished carting everything out of the garage but he did his best to ignore it and to be helpful by holding things in place while his dad cut, then fitted the shelves. Cody watched his dad's comb over flop up and down in cadence with the thrust and pull motions as he sawed through each plank of wood and tried not to compare the obvious sinew of his father's biceps to his own undefined upper arms. *Least I still have plenty of hair* he thought and ran his hand up and over his forehead to pull it away from his eyes. *Going to have to get it cut soon.*

When his dad had the shelves rigged out to his satisfaction Cody brought everything back into the garage, handing each item to his father so he could fussily place them just so on the new shelves.

'Looks good, eh boy?' His father said as he admired the finished space.

'Reckon so!'

'Good space to work on my ships.' His father ran his hand over the one empty shelf that reached to the top of his waist.

'Nice and dry.' Cody agreed. His dad could work on his hobby of putting ships in bottles from the relative comfort of inside the garage on foul weather days instead of in the back yard and only during good weather as had been his habit now for many years. He didn't like to work on his models-in-progress indoors as he was convinced that Cody or Betty would somehow damage the delicate structures. However, Betty was expected to dust the finished models, which Edward had arranged into a proud display on shelves in the living room.

'What time is mum coming home tomorrow?' Cody said at last.

'And here I was hoping you'd offer to make us a cup of coffee.' His dad snapped in response.

'Only asked a simple question.' Cody muttered as he stomped off towards the house.

A loud crash stopped him in his tracks and he looked back over his shoulder to see his father was standing over the remnants of one of his models, head hanging down, looking as broken as boat and bottle before him. Suddenly his head whipped around, eyes blazing into Cody's 'Get in that house and make me a coffee already!'

Cody got his dad a cup of coffee and they worked until his dad decided it was time for supper. Their hard work that day had given Cody and Edward enormous appetites and they shared the remainder of a loaf of bread shrouded in an uncomfortable silence as they moped up the dregs of the stew pot. After watching a repeat of the movie 'Rawhide' with his dad, Cody went upstairs to have a bath. He fell asleep that night with left hand resting on top of his covers so that he didn't roll over on his sore finger in the night.

Mum'll be home sometime today was Cody's first thought on waking Sunday morning. It would be nice to have someone in the house to speak to besides his father who had become even more of a curmudgeon over the past few days; an accomplishment Cody would not have thought possible if he had not endured it first-hand. He stayed in bed long after he woke waiting for his dad to get up, hoping Edward would go out to visit Sandy and George as his parents usually did on a Sunday morning. Once his dad got up Cody listened to him clattering round downstairs until he heard the kettle click on for the third time before he admitted defeat and got out of bed and into his clothes; his dad would have left by now if he was going to.

'Moaning.' his dad said, which was the closest he ever came to attempting humour though he looked anything but smiley this morning.

'Morn'in dad.'

'Cuppa?' asked Edward as he nosily clanged his spoon round his own mug.

'Please.' Cody sat down at the kitchen table, passing the palm of his hand over the familiar pitted surface. His dad sat down, placing Cody's mug beside his own. Cody looked up puzzled and began to reach across the table for it, stopping when he noticed the slim gold band cradled in his father's palm where it rested between the two mugs.

'That looks like mum's?' Cody cradled his mug of tea between his palms.

'You'd be right.' His dad swept his finger gently round and round the circle of gold.

'Is she back then?' Hope lifted his voice then he took a drink of his scalding tea.

'She won't be back son, I found this in my beside table drawer.'

'Why'd she leave it there?'

'To tell me she wasn't coming back, that she doesn't want her ring because she doesn't want me!' Edward's voice rose to a shout on the final word. Sadness making his facial muscles ripple, his temper shortened even further by the grief inside. He stood up, shoved the ring deep into his front pocket, and after putting on his shoes grabbed his mug and slammed the door on his way out.

Unsure what to do next Cody drank his tea for a couple of minutes and then stood up, bewildered tears filling his eyes. He poured his tea down the kitchen sink then looked out the kitchen window. His dad was stomping towards the car, toolbox in hand. *Dad must be wrong, mum wouldn't leave without saying goodbye to me, wouldn't leave me here on my own with him*, Cody thought. Then, with a sinking heart, Cody replayed their last conversation and realised that his mum had said goodbye after she had hugged him. In a vile mood he set about tidying the house. He ran a cloth over all of the ornaments except for his father's model ships and was sulkily sweeping the kitchen floor, burning with anger over his father's part in scaring his mother away, when his father burst violently in through the back door.

'Cody, get me some water, quick.'

'What for?'

'Don't question me boy, just do it! I've swallowed something that poured out of the engine and it tasted like gas!'

Without thinking, Cody grabbed his father's cigarette lighter from the table and handed them to him. 'Rule two Dad, do us all a favour why don't you?' Cody regretted the words as soon as they

23

left his mouth, talk like that meant he was no better than the man he'd grown to resent for the very same reason.

'Cody!' The colour on his father's face drained, then flared back a furious red, convincing Cody that whatever bit of love his dad had held within for his son had now been destroyed. Edward made his way to the sink, turned the tap on, filling and then emptying his mouth into the sink several times. He dried his face on the tea towel, carefully folding it back over the oven door handle before making his way towards the stairs casting an empty look in Cody's direction as he passed.

Cody glanced down at his shoes embarrassed that he hadn't at least tried to make amends by handing his dad the tea towel. 'Dad, I...'

'Don't bother Cody, I think you've said more than enough.' Edward's eyes looked empty; haunted by the love he'd lost.

Cody fled the house in shame and ended up at Lizzie and Charles where he begged them to put him up for the night. 'I know I can't go home again because I'm scared of myself... of the way I feel when I am around him now that mum's gone. Do you think mum'll come back sis?'

'You and dad have always been at loggerheads. You've managed to keep rubbing along together just fine till now and you'll need each other even more now that mum's gone.' Lizzie sighed. 'And, she's not coming back,' She finished seeing the look on Cody's face.

'How do you know for sure?' Cody demanded angrily.

'She left her wedding ring, Cody. That says a lot.'

'Well maybe she just took it off for some reason and forgot to put it back on before she left? She always takes it off when she makes pastry!' Cody's face crumpled and quivered as he fought back tears.

'Did she leave any pastry for you and dad?'

Cody shook his head. 'Just stew,' he said in a defeated voice. 'It's dad's fault she didn't tell me she was going, she's too scared of him finding out where she is!'

'Maybe she didn't say anything to you because she knew that if you begged her to stay she wouldn't be able to keep her resolve to leave. She knows you're capable of looking after yourself Cody, and if she didn't leave when she did, then she may never have had another chance. That's what I think anyway and I'm sure mum'll be in touch soon.'

Cody lifted his head in time to see Lizzie and Charles exchange a glance before Charles spoke in a firm voice, 'You can sleep on our sofa tonight if you like Cody, but there's not enough room in our house even for the two of us so you wont be able to stay any longer than overnight. You'll have to head on back to your dad's after work tomorrow.'

'If mum's not going back there then neither am I!' Cody wrapped his arms round himself and to his shame began bawling like a baby.

'Then you'll have to go to Sandy and George's. I'll put the kettle on.' Charles left the room hastily. Lizzie settled herself beside Cody and wrapped her arms round him, drawing him close, murmuring gentle, unintelligible sounds of comfort, until Cody managed to compose himself enough to drink the tea that Charles had made.

~ ~

As Cody lay in the darkened front room his mind whirled. How could his mum think he needed looking after? He had stayed living at home so she wouldn't have to be on her own with his dad! He grunted with embarrassment that he hadn't mentioned this to Lizzie when she told him why she thought his mum had felt she needed to leave without saying goodbye. He pulled the thin cover further up his chest and then lay silent as Charles's voice drifted through the bedroom on the other side of the wall.

'I hope Cody takes me seriously Lizzie, otherwise we'll be stuck with him like an unwanted child.'

'I'm sorry darling; he doesn't mean to be a bother, he's just young and confused. He can't go to Sandy and George's, you do know that, don't you? Not with…' Lizzie's soft clear voice was interrupted by her husband's louder one.

'Well I think it's high time Cody grew up and moved out on his own actually.'

Cody could hear the springs on their bed creak as one or both of them sat down.

'He and dad have never seen eye to eye and Cody worries about mum…we all do!' Lizzie's voice melted away from its fierce finish into tense silence that Cody could almost feel.

'Not your problem anymore darling, you've got your own household to manage, and I couldn't ask for a better wife or a happier home. I wouldn't like to see it change. I'd have left that shit hole of a home life years ago, and Cody needs to make his own way into the world just like you did.'

Cody made a face at the wall as Charles finished speaking.

'I couldn't have done it without you Charles. I'll try not to let my worries about Cody and mum interfere with what we have here.' Lizzie's voice was apologetic.

Cody turned away from the wall and pulled his pillow up over his exposed ear.

No one slept well that night. Charles and Lizzie fretted for hours in whispered staccato that leaked through the wall in incomprehensible but still audible drips, and Cody gave up on any pretence of sleep and instead thought long into the night. His eyes were dry from the tears he had shed earlier and his pride drowned in waves of shame over having cried in front of his sister and Charles. Thinking over his childhood brought fresh tears; by the time he had started school he had already lost the innate ability to be naturally optimistic, to instinctively believe that he had the potential to be anyone and to do anything. His mother had called him a worrywart from a young age and with good reason. He had struggled to make friends, and the few boys at school who would tolerate him soon drifted away once they had graduated and moved away to go to university. The one person that Cody had been confident was a reliable, trustworthy and constant presence in his life had been his mother. Despite his constant fretting, he had never imagined that one day his mother would run away and abandon him with his father, and he knew his grief was all the more intense because he'd not been able to prepare for this loss. *Rule three: don't be a loser, eh dad?* Cody thought fiercely. *Well, we're both losers now!*

Cody couldn't see beyond this moment but he did know that he couldn't go back to the life he had been living, and that he did not want to end up an angry, abandoned, misogynistic man like his father. *From now on I will live each day without worrying about all the tomorrows to come.* He closed his eyes against the advancing dawn and slept.

Chapter four – Moonstone

The next day Cody woke tired but filled with the resolve to set off on his own and try to grow into the person he believed he wanted to become. He waited until he heard Charles leave, then splashed water on his face, scrubbed toothpaste over his teeth using his finger, and declined Lizzie's offer of breakfast.

'Got to get to work.' He gave a weak smile in response to the tired one his sister offered.

'You okay now Cody?'

'I know I need to make some changes. I'll be in touch.' He exchanged an awkward hug with his sister and headed out the door.

~ ~

'Give this to Mike for me wud'ja?' Cody said as he placed his letter of resignation on the secretary's desk.

'Give me what?' Mike said poking his head around the corner of his office.

Cody hung his head and refused to answer.

'In you come Cody. I won't be losing one of my best men without good reason!'

Cody slunk around the secretary's desk and slouched himself into the chair facing Mike's.

'You get a fright when you hurt yerself last week?'

Cody shook his head and maintained eye contact with his boots.

'We done anything to make you want to leave?'

Cody managed a grunt of dissent, afraid to try and speak around the unexpected lump in his throat. He had enjoyed his time at the sawmill and wondered if he was throwing away the last of his pride by leaving.

Mike tapped the side of his pen nib against his desk blotter. 'I can see you're upset, and I want you to feel free to speak your mind.'

'I've said all I'm sayin' 'bout my reasons for leavin', sir.' Cody kept his eyes fixed on his bandaged finger that rested on his leg.

'Well I'm not havin' you walk out of this job without a letter of reference to take with you.'

Cody drank a cup of muddy coffee heavily loaded with sugar cradled between his shaking hands while the secretary typed out the foreman's scrawled words of recommendation.

'Take care of that finger of yours, and of yourself. Don't hesitate to come back if you're looking for work.' He said as he handed Cody the envelope containing his signed letter of reference. *Girl trouble* he decided *that's got to be the reason for the boy's sudden departure*.

'I will sir, and thank you for everything you've taught me.' Cody knew it was time to beat a hasty retreat out of the sawmill office before he embarrassed himself by blubbing in front of his former boss. He shoved the letter into the pocket of his jeans as he walked to the bank.

'I'd like to empty my account please.'

'You'll need to leave a balance of one dollar to keep your account open, would you like to do that?'

'Can I use my account anywhere?'

'As long as you have your account details.'

'Yes in that case I'd like to keep my account open thanks.'

'Going somewhere exciting?'

'No idea.' Cody said enigmatically.

The teller took the hint and got busy counting out the savings Cody had managed to accumulate after paying out for his room and board each week at his parents' house. The total balance wasn't much but Cody figured that if he was frugal then it would be enough for his needs till he got another job.

Knowing his father would already be at work, Cody took a chance and went home to get the few things he didn't want to leave without. Cody had always enjoyed the freshness of this time of year and as he cut through the park he walked slowly, taking in the display of bright flowers and the almost neon green of the new leaves which were just beginning to unfurl on the branches. The spring air was light and bright, a promise of the gentle heat to come later in the day. He opened the front door cautiously; his shoulders tense until the cool, silent house announced that his father was at work. Cody relaxed enough to slather thick slices of the bread he had bought on the way home with butter and jam. Eating the food in huge bites he washed them down with a large mug of hot milky tea. As the warmth spread through him, Cody's eyes welled with tears that he swiped away with the back of his hand. After a quick bath he began mimicking his mother's moves a few days previously; throwing his items of choice into the large canvas bag he found on the top of his father's wardrobe, there was a folded map inside which he transferred to the back pocket of his jeans. Cody packed his sturdy work boots and all his clothing, which didn't amount to much, and hardly made a discernable bulge in the bag. He placed The Moonstone by Wilkie Collins on top of this meagre cushion of clothes. It was his favourite novel, a treasured gift from his mum who had first read it when she was in her late teens. When the local library had held its annual sale of old books his mum had been delighted to find a slightly worn copy that she bought for Cody, Sandy and Lizzie to share.

Neither of his sisters were much interested in reading more than the occasional short story to be found within the weekly women's magazine they shared so the book ended up as Cody's own by default. Cody often wondered where his copy had been in its life. It had been printed in the US in 1900 and still had the original paper wrapper over the hard cover, which the library had then protected with faintly stripped plain brown parcel paper. He had read it several times in the past six years and was still enraptured by the richly layered multiple narratives; partaking by proxy in the experiences of diamond smuggling, drug abuse, romance and suicide. It allowed him to escape into a world much more exciting than the drudge that his own life had already become. Cody had whole chapters memorised and would often dream of them with himself mixed into the storyline in myriad ways. He packed it along with his other belongings because he thought it would come in handy for the long bus trip ahead. Cody looked around the four yellowing walls that framed his room; his bed butted up against the wall opposite his door, his single wardrobe to the left and window framed by thin curtains to the right. He hadn't accumulated much in his twenty-two years really; positivity, contentment and peace of mind had never come naturally to Cody and he hadn't experienced any material wealth either. His bedding, a few stacked comics on the top shelf of his wardrobe, his clothes and book, which were already in the bag. He took his winter coat off its hangar and folded it before placing it too in the bag; he wasn't planning on coming back so he would need it come winter. Feeling his chest swell with renewed angst, he tucked a black and white photograph of his parents on their wedding day inside the pages of The Moonstone. His mother looked radiantly happy and slim with no hint of the fact that she was already four months pregnant with Sandy and his father looked young and determined. Next to that he placed a colour photo of himself sat on their front steps with Sandy and Lizzie on either side, squinting into the sunshine, their mouths smeared with the ice cream they were eating. Cody could remember the feel of the warm ice cream trickling down over his thumb and the sound of his mother's laugh as she urged them to hurry and eat it before it melted away completely. A fleeting longing to relive that day was soon banished by several less pleasant memories in which his father's grumpiness featured. *I am doing the right thing by leaving* he reassured himself. He placed a towel and soap wrapped in a flannel into his bag before tightening the cord that ran through the steel lined holes in a circle around the opening. He opened the cedar wood chest at the foot of his parents' bed intending to get another blanket but stopped short when he saw the pink quilt which Cody had seen packed in his mom's suitcase. He straightened as his stomach ran cold. *It's like she left most of herself here* Cody slung the bag over his shoulder and, after a last look around his room as he passed it he made his way downstairs, forcing away all feelings of regret over leaving the pink quilt in its chest. He stopped in the kitchen to add the rest of the loaf of bread onto which he spread butter, peanut butter and jam, a few apples and some cheese to his provisions. Digging through the junk drawer he found a pad of paper and a pencil and left his father a note:

I am fed up of living under your rules but I'm sorry for the way I treated you yesterday. I'm leaving home so you don't have to worry about it happening again. Cody

Cody struggled to think of a way to explain all of the emotions churning around inside him but decided that what he had written in the note would have to do for now; maybe Lizzie would fill in the blanks in the note he had written his father.

Sandy, I have left home. Lizzie will explain. I will write again when I am settled. Your brother, Cody.

He folded the note to Sandy into an envelope, sealed it and wrote her name on the front. He tucked the envelope into his pocket and paused partway through slinging the duffle bag over his shoulder. Taking the stairs two at a time he lifted the unfinished pink quilt from the blanket box and placed it on top of the other things he was taking with him.

He tied the bag tightly shut, slung it over his shoulder, grabbed his straw Stetson from its hook, closed the front door softly behind him and walked to the bus station.

Chapter five – Ganderbrook

He walked to the mailbox at the end of Sandy's road, pushed the letter in, then squared his shoulders and walked to the bus station. Cody spent a few minutes searching the list of destinations for the day's scheduled departures before deciding to buy a ticket to Lumen's Gate. The map showed it to be a small town and that the scheduled stops before it would mean the bus would take several hours to get to it. As an added bonus, it was also as far as he could get for the money he was willing to spend. Cody shoved the bus ticket into the front pocket of his shirt and he made his way to the correct platform. He stood on his own in the warm spring air with his bag between his feet and waited patiently for his transport to arrive. He had decided the night before that he'd had enough of living in a big city and dreamed of the simpler life he imagined he would find in a rural area. By the time the bus pulled up a few other passengers had begun to gather though not many for such a large vehicle.

The driver hopped down off the bottom step and shut the door behind him. 'I'll be back in twenty minutes,' he said the assembled people in response to the expectant look on their faces and sauntered off in the direction of the station diner.

Cody decided he had best go to the toilet before starting the journey and, slinging his bag over his shoulder, he made his way back into the bus station. He emptied his bladder, washed his hands, cupped them and drank several handfuls of water. After he had slaked his thirst he made a detour into the diner and bought a newspaper and a bar of chocolate. Certain he was now fully prepared for the journey ahead he went back to take up his position on the platform again. Eventually the driver strolled over with a toothpick tucked in the corner of his mouth. The assembled passengers shuffled over expectantly as the driver popped open the seal on the luggage hold and watched as he stored their bags. Once he'd finished this task he opened the door and collected their tickets as they entered the bus and made themselves comfortable. Cody chose a seat halfway along the bus and looked out the window at nothing in particular until the bus had finished reversing out of the station. As soon as they began moving through the city Cody opened his paper and began reading. It wasn't long before he felt his eyes closing, the movement of the bus was soothing and the lack of sleep from the night before was catching up with him. Cody folded his newspaper, placed it between the window and his head, and rested his hands on his lap, careful to place his tender finger topmost before he succumbed to the call of his dreams.

Cody drifted in and out of consciousness dragging fragments of his anxious dreams with him from the ether of sleep, mulling over them, eyes firmly closed. The bus made a stop at another station forty-five minutes into the journey to pick up a few passengers but Cody kept his eyes closed knowing from the schedule that it was only a quick break along the route. He was vaguely aware of the not unpleasant sensation of the top edge of his seat gently scratching at his temple and the random sounds of the other passengers until he was lulled back into much deeper relaxation by the gentle vibrations coming through his seat. Eventually Cody slept deeply, and for a while he knew no more angst as even the niggling twinges of his healing finger were displaced by the restorative oblivion.

~ ~

'Benchling! One hour rest stop!' The driver announced as the bus shuddered to a stop. Cody dragged himself up from the depths of his dreams. He placed his slightly smudged newspaper on the seat before scrubbing his face with his hands until he felt refreshed. This act of dry washing also served to surreptitiously remove the traces of newsprint as well as the remnants of the drooled and now sticky salvia that had almost but not quite dried. Cody cringed inwardly and hoped the woman who had been sat opposite hadn't noticed, though he wasn't quite certain why it should matter to him if she had. He stood, pausing to tense and relax his stiff legs in an attempt to loosen the muscles before moving out into the aisle. Cody freshened up in the washroom, thought fleetingly of the food and chocolate bar that he'd packed in his bag, which was now stowed in the compartment under the bus and joined the queue for seats in the diner attached to the station. It was about the same size as the one in Cordbridge, which made him think that Benchling must be a decent sized city too. After growing up in the relative anonymity of a city, he was glad not to be doing more than stopping here.

Cody longed for what he imagined would be a caring community atmosphere of a rural town, which was another reason he had chosen Lumen's Gate. The woman selling the bus tickets had happened to mention that it was small town and sat on the edge of the apple-growing belt. Cody had reckoned he would be able to find work at one of the orchards and, in keeping with his new no-worry mind-set, decided that he would think about what to do for work in the winter closer to the time. He took a seat at the counter and ordered sausage, eggs, chips and beans. Savouring every greasy bite he wiped his plate dry with his buttered slice of bread. Cody knew there was no point rushing back to the bus as he could see the driver still sat at the far end of the counter, so he took his time, lingering over his mug of strong coffee as he alternated between reading his paper and watching the two cooks sweating over the grill and barking orders to the busy waitresses over the noise of the frying food and customers' conversation. Suddenly Cody realised that the noise level had dropped significantly in the diner. Heart racing as he realised he was unsure of how much time had passed, he whipped his head round to look for the bus driver who was no longer in the diner. Cody hastily shuffled his paper together, wondering if he'd missed the departure announcement and rushed to the bus. The driver was assisting an elderly woman up onto the steps of the bus.

'Thought I'd come out to find you'd already left.' he said with relief.

'Nah you've made it with ten minutes to spare.'

Cody stepped up onto the bus noticing that there were several more people on board now. He found the seat he'd sat in earlier still empty and settled in against the window, randomly eavesdropping on the conversations flowing around him.

'Oh no I simply can't use more than two needles when making a sweater, I have to do one section at a time the old fashioned way, using only two needles or I end up dropping whole rows of stitches.'

'I haven't looked back since I discovered circular needles, you really should try them.'

'And then Harry told me that if I even so much as thought about...'

'Clayey soil works wonders for keeping pumpkin plants under control and it holds the wet in too.'

'I wish I'd thought to go to the men's room before we left.'

'That's your age that is.'

'The forgetting to go or the wanting to go all the time?'

'It's been warm this spring, 'spect that means we'll have a wet summer.'

'Makes for good apple growing that though eh? Wet nights and warm days makes for nice, sweet plump apples.'

'Yeah 'n' corn on the cob too.'

'Well I think your husband is a fool not to appreciate you more.'

'Feelin' my age nowadays, why I can remember a time when I could work all day and drink all night. '

'Took me years to train that coon hound and then he just upped and died on me!'

'Tragic, that was, proper sad.'

'Time to start creosoting those fence panels before the spring rot sets in deep.'

'Wish someone had told me those late raspberries spread like weeds!'

As Cody listened he wondered what links these people had with each other. Husband and wife? Friends? Siblings? Parent and child? Bored businessman passing the time by flirting with a lone woman? An unexpected surge of aloneness passed over him as he realised that he had left all those links behind in Cordbridge.

S'okay, Cody reassured himself, *what I don't have can't be taken away. And, it can't leave me*, he thought as an image of his mother flashed across his mind.

The bus driver pulled the door shut and plonked himself down into his seat.

Another two and a half hour's worth of travelling with one quick stop along the way and he would be at Lumen's gate. Cody looked out the window, forcing himself away from the painful thoughts of what he had lost so far in his life. He was quickly mesmerised by the beauty unravelling at speed outside the bus. They had left the city of Benchling behind after only a few minutes' driving. The rolling hills were unfurling into a seemingly unending stretch of meadow filled valley. Cows and horses were dotted about the landscape, idly grazing or resting on the ground busily chewing their cud, the farmhouses and outbuildings almost camouflaged by the landscape. Eventually they began to pass by houses, their growing numbers indicating the approach to a town called Ganderbrook according to the dusty roadside sign.

Chapter six – Bajamawammers

The bus slowed then pulled off the road coming to a stop outside a one pump fuel station where a young woman stood waiting. Cody watched with interest as she bent over to pick up her case. Her long hair fell forward to drop in a shimmering sheet over her shoulder, obscuring her face until she straightened and flicked it back with a toss of her head, revealing delicate features which matched her slight build. The only discordant aspects were her large breasts.

That's a great pair of bajamawammers, Cody thought before realising he was staring and forced his eyes away. The driver disembarked and Cody could hear him bantering with her as he stowed her case in the compartment between the wheels. She virtually bounced up the steps onto the bus, pausing as she cast a glance along the row of seats looking for an empty space before spotting the one next to Cody. She flashed him an expansive smile and began moving towards him. Cody responded by glancing down and clearing his paper off the otherwise empty seat. He felt flustered by the opportunity before him. What would he find to say to such a confident, pretty woman if she did sit beside him?

It doesn't matter really he told himself *I've got less than two hours left of my journey and I'm certainly not looking to start a relationship, quite the opposite in fact*, he told himself firmly, despite primal instinct making him want to encourage her to smile at him like that again; for forever if possible.

Cody looked up when he sensed that she had paused in the aisle beside him.

'Erm, do you mind if I sit here?'

'No! Uh yes, please!' Cody, flustered, stopped and then tried again. 'Yes, that's fine. Thanks.' His cheeks flamed red. *Is it my imagination or has everyone stopped talking so they can listen to me splutter like a fool*? Cody wondered as he forced his eyes to face the seat in front in order to avoid staring at the woman beside him. She smelled fresh, sweet and crisp, like a green apple or fresh mown grass. *I'd like to roll in the grass with her* he thought inanely then admonished himself *like she'd let a loser like you!* He fiddled with his paper and ended up tucking it between the seat and side of the bus. A slim hand popped into his line of vision.

'My name's Ellen.'

'Cody.'

'My brother's middle name is Cody!'

'Oh. Uh, it's a pretty common name I guess?' Cody could hear the noise levels rise all around them as the bus pulled away and the others carried on their conversations.

'Yeah maybe.' Ellen stopped and waited expectantly.

Cody smiled at her uncertainly.

'I'm going to stay with my brother and sister in law for a while. To help out. She's having a baby!' Ellen exuberantly filled in the gaps in their conversation.

'Oh! I wouldn't know what to do with a baby.'

'Don't you have any younger brothers or sisters?'

'Nope, I'm the baby of the family.' Cody forced a smile and banished thoughts of his family firmly away.

'Where you going?'

'Lumen's Gate.'

'That place is smaller than Ganderbrook! You got family there?'

'Nope just drifting around, hoping to get some work on one of the apple farms, maybe move on after harvest time, maybe not. All depends on how I like small town living.'

'I hate it.' Ellen said decisively. 'Spent my whole life living in a town where everyone knows my business. I want to get a job as a secretary or maybe a librarian when my sister in law doesn't need my help as much. That way I wont have to move back to Ganderbrook.'

'I'm the opposite. Grew up in Cordbridge and I'm happy to be escaping the anonymity of city life. In the city you're just a number on the street, a face amongst hundreds of others. I want to experience living in a community where everyone knows my name.'

The old adage that opposites attract proved true for Ellen and Cody. He filled her in on what she could expect from city life and Ellen told Cody tales of rural life. Her textured voice enriched his senses, dropping into his ears in melodic layers, and the last leg of his journey to Lumen's Gate passed faster than he would have liked. *Best this way*, he thought to himself. *Any longer with Ellen and I'll want to follow her like a well trained dog except that I'm done with getting attached to people.*

'Wanna swap addresses?' Ellen said as if she could read his mind and was determined to thwart any ideas he had of not getting attached to her.

'I don't know what mine will be.' Cody quickly countered.

'Oh that's ok, I'll give you my brother's address and you can write or phone with yours as soon as you're settled.' Ellen said confidently.

'Sure that's a good idea.' Cody said, not wanting to hurt her feelings. He told himself that he would throw away her address as soon as he was out of her sight. *No point setting myself up to fail*, he thought. *She'd soon lose interest once she got to know me and I've had enough heartbreak to last a lifetime.*

All too soon the bus slowed and then pulled over onto the roadside. Ellen stood to let him out into the aisle then sat down in his seat by the window. Cody smiled at her and made a show of tucking his bus ticket, on which she'd written her contact details, into his wallet.

'Bye for now,' Ellen said in a quiet voice as she stared at him intensely.

'Be seeing ya.' Cody said, not meaning it until he saw how her face lit up at his words. *Maybe*, he thought, *I'll send her a note during the summer, just to say hello.*

Chapter seven - Randall's

Cody stepped down into watery late afternoon sunshine; the bus driver released his bag from the hold, got back on, honked the horn and drove off. Cody returned Ellen's wave and then looked at his surroundings. Miles of open blue sky and fields to the sides and behind, and in front of him down a long road lined with dusty gravel stretched the town of Lumen's Gate. He began walking; passing a hardware store, bank, post office, barber, corner shop, butcher, grocery store, and assorted other businesses vital to the smooth function of a small town before he crossed the road and went back the way he'd just come, passing a greengrocer, hair salon, hotel, library and a tiny crowded cafe. In what seemed very little time Cody reached the end of the pavement.

One more step and I'll be on my way back out of town, which actually wouldn't be a bad idea, he thought, *if only I had a car.* Cody sighed, aware of his finger dully aching, as he turned round to look at the buildings lining the street he'd just walked down. The small hotel covered in grey cedar shingles and fronted with the word *Randall's* hand painted onto a warped wooden sign would have to do, as it was the only place that offered rooms for rent. The porch steps creaked as they settled under his feet, waking the mangy looking thin dog lying to one side of the door.

The dog raised its head slowly, panting and then took a hopeful lick inside a container that looked as if it had been a plastic bucket in a former life and was now roughly cut down to bowl depth. The dog looked intently at the newcomer and then huffed hopefully at Cody who said 'Hey fella' and bent down to rub behind his crumpled matted ears for a moment before opening the door. Halfway through the door he paused and leaned back to pick up what he assumed was the dog's water bowl. As his eyes adjusted to the interior lighting, Cody realised that the lumpy shadow in the centre of his line of vision was a sour looking man. He moved towards him, reluctantly absorbing the sight of the day's growth of beard and a lifetime's accumulation of grime plastered on the man's face.

A disturbing sense of déjà vu descended on Cody rendering him incapable of saying more than 'I need a room erm uh sir?' He cringed at how feeble his voice sounded.

The clerk scratched at his beard, kept his eyes lowered and flicked a page over in the magazine he was reading.

Cody tried again. 'That dog of yours seems thirsty.' He plonked the dog bowl onto the counter and stood there, quietly hopeful until the clerk finally acknowledged his presence.

'Yeah we got a room.'

'That'll do,' Cody grunted past the almost palpable smell of the clerk's foul breath.

'Ain't my mutt, ain't no ones, sure don't want him here.' He glared at the water bowl before snatching it up, stomping away to fill it with water and deposit it roughly on the porch.

'Poor dog's done no wrong, has he?'

'You ain't got no right to talk down to me son, you'd best be 'membering that.'

Cody thought *rule three time*, squared his shoulders and said, 'Sorry sir, just don't like to see an animal without water in this heat and all. I'll get it myself next time.' His words sounded more confident than he felt.

Moist bottom lip hanging down, the clerk pushed a grubby, well-thumbed register across the scratched wood and handed Cody a pen with the top chewed soft. It looked wet.

'Some folks talk in this town...'

''Bout what?' Cody handed the pen back being careful to hold it at the very bottom only.

'Like to say the room's haunted.'

'Why's that?'

'On account of old man Stanton killing his'self there.'

'Well I reckon he's got better things to be doing now than hanging round a room that was awful enough to want to die in.' Cody shrugged with feigned indifference and held out his hand for the key.

'Yep likely so. Room's down the hall to your right.'

The key came attached to a block of wood the size of a brick, room number painted unevenly on it. Cody made his way down the hall, pausing to glance in the bar. The antlers hung above the door gave the room a macabre, uninviting atmosphere. What was he doing here?

'Chasing the greener grass,' he muttered. Perhaps emptying his bank account and buying a bus ticket to take him as far away as he could afford had been a big mistake. Or perhaps it hadn't, but Cody knew one thing for sure, he had never felt lonelier in his life.

Cody averted his eyes from the bony display above the bar and pushed the door of his room open. He flicked the light on, then off, preferring the look of the room when it was shrouded in thin shadows. He stood still for a moment, enjoying the fleeting silence that always came to him for a few seconds after he had stopped moving, until his ears stopped expecting the sound of his footfall and began to focus on other noises. A streaked window in the far wall overlooked the street. He glanced at the few items in the room; the dented iron frame, which was doing a poor job of supporting the mattress, the scratched chest of drawers with the cloudy mirror hung directly above, the stained sink and the worn rug. A scarred wooden door hid a toilet and pigmy sized bathtub, the porcelain of both pitted and stained with age.

Tired enough for the bed to look inviting, Cody slid the duffle bag off his shoulder, dropped it at his feet and hooked his hat on the back of the door. Walking over to the bed he stood rubbing the feel of hat off his head, and stared a while at the cheap print depicting a buffalo hunt. The magnificent beasts were massive but no match for an attack by those mounted on the horses. Their carefully grown horns, so lethal when used against any natural enemy, were no use in protecting them against the guns' power. Cody slipped a finger behind the frame and gave it an experimental tug before lifting if off the wall hook and sliding it under his bed. He sat and then flopped back onto the bed, propped his boot clad feet up on the footboard, and dropped his head with a grateful sigh onto the thin pillow.

He lay, his mind drifting, until he felt something tickle his hand. Glancing to his left, he noticed a large spider making its way across his hand. He shook it off; grimacing with distaste at the tingly feeling the contact of its feet had left on his skin. The 'heebie jeebies' he would have described it, if anyone had been there to enquire at his reaction. He rubbed his hand briskly and that sensation overrode the last traces of the spider vibes. Cody saw movement in his peripheral vision and looking down he saw that the spider had returned and was now making its way along his legs.

'Urgh, gerroff!' he groused, flicking it with his fingers.

The spider persisted until Cody grudgingly sat up so that the spider could trundle its way along the bed, over the side, abseiling the last few feet from the edge of the counterpane to the floor and finally disappearing into a large crack that ran along between the wall and floor at the far edge of the room. The spider clearly had firm views on what constituted his territory and his home and was determined to persist until he had made it safely there.

As he lay there on that sagging bed in an unfamiliar town he was washed with the familiar fug of loneliness, and Cody wished he had hugged his mom back when she'd wrapped her arms round him on Friday. Only three days ago and it felt like a lifetime had passed. *Which in a way it has*, Cody thought, *I've left my old life behind.* An image of the dog on the hotel porch flashed across his mind and just before he fell asleep Cody impulsively broke his new life rule and decided he'd make him his own. He slept until the chill in the room reached deeply enough in to pull him from his dreams. Pulling his boots off, Cody got under the covers with his clothes on, and lay wide-awake trying to make plans for his future until he warmed up enough to fall asleep again.

Chapter eight – Jake

Cody spent a restless night fidgeting on the lumpy mattress, trying to keep himself out of the deep dent in the middle because it made him feel vaguely claustrophobic. The noise from the bar didn't help; moderately loud Outlaw country music and drunken conversations spoken at full volume with occasional shouting thrown in for punctuation, drifted all too easily through the thin door of his room. By daybreak he was exhausted but wide-awake and waiting for an excuse to get up. Slinging his legs over the side he sat on the edge, sock covered feet flat on the floor, while he tried to decide what to do. His stomach rumbled loudly reminding him that he hadn't eaten since yesterday afternoon. He'd gone to sleep without brushing his teeth or having a drink and his mouth now tasted like a septic tank. The desire for food was bordering on painful, but first he needed to get his mouth clean. He knew he would be sick if he tried to chew food while his mouth was in this state. Cody shoved himself upright using his hands as a lever and the mattress as a springboard. Rummaging around in his bag he found his toothbrush and paste, a face cloth, soap and towel. He brushed his teeth vigorously, scrapping away at his tongue with the bristles until he nearly gagged, then temporarily fooled his belly into feeling full by drinking copious amounts of water from the scratched glass he found on the sink. His urge to eat eased slightly and Cody decided to bathe while he was still in the bathroom. He wanted to get downstairs and find out more about that dog on the porch and he reasoned that once he'd eaten he would want to go straight away. Best to get his ablutions out of the way before food and then there would be nothing holding him back from making that dog part of his new life. He couldn't figure out what it was about the dog that appealed to him so. He'd never considered himself a 'dog person', quite the opposite in fact because he had always made a fuss of any cat he passed but never so much had an urge to pat a dog.

This one looked so lonely that his heart might just break and that's what got to me Cody decided.

Cody could hear the rain pounding against the window in his room as he lowered himself into the bath and he was glad the dog had the porch roof to provide some sort of shelter against the wet. He tried not to think about the rain coming through the porch railings and concentrated on getting washed, using soap lather on his hair as well as his body. As he dried off he decided he couldn't wait any longer to eat, he would have to shave later on during the day. Standing with his towel wrapped round his waist, Cody chewed huge bites of the peanut butter and jelly sandwiches he'd made yesterday. The cheese looked greasy and felt soft so Cody regretfully threw it away, finishing his breakfast with an apple instead. He dressed in clean underwear but otherwise put back on the same clothes he had on yesterday. *They aren't dirty* he reasoned with himself, *all I did was sit in them all day while I travelled here.* He tucked yesterday's underwear aside to be hand washed later and looked out the window. The rain had eased and although the sky looked grey and flat with the promise of more rain, the town looked refreshed now that the wet surfaces had sheen to them.

He checked his watch; 8:04am, time to head to the reception and find out more about the dog on the porch. He placed his hat on his head and locked the door behind him. He spent a few minutes loitering outside his room while he tried to decide where to put the key with its huge wood block before settling on shoving the block into the back pocket of his jeans. The key clunked against the block on the other side of his jean pocket as he walked past the bar door which was shut making the hallway seem smaller and the antlers loom menacingly. A woman, who except for the obvious gender difference, looked almost exactly like the curmudgeon from yesterday, was sat behind the reception desk.

'Good morning M'am.' Cody said politely as he removed his hat, hoping to make a better impression on her than he had with the man yesterday.

'Call me Belinda! I'm too young to be called M'am.'

Cody was astonished to find a raised eyebrow could appear so threatening.

Belinda continued, 'Well it's morning all right, not sure it's a good one though.' She grumpily gestured towards the view through the window. 'Plays my joints up something fierce this weather does.'

'My gran used to wrap baked potatoes in towels and place them on her aching joints.'

'That's an excellent and frugal idea. The heat would last a long time and I could re-bake the potatoes if I need to. Thanks for the tip.' Her face shifted uncomfortably until it had rearranged itself into a semblance of a smile.

'That dog on the porch?'

'Oh that scruffy smelly hound! He just showed up last week, no idea who he belongs to, certainly no one in 'Gate.'

'The man behind reception yesterday,' Cody began.

'That was my brother, Howard. There's just the two of us on reception and we've run this hotel since we were old enough to see over the counter.'

'My...that's quite an accomplishment.' Cody managed to fumble out what he hoped was an appropriate response.

'Why you asking about that dog?'

'Well your brother said the same as you, that the dog doesn't belong to anyone, which got me thinking that I'd be happy to take him off your hands.'

'You cain't have him in yer room, we've got standards to maintain.'

'I understand.' Cody lied because he couldn't see how the dog could make his room look any worse. 'Could he stay on the porch as long as I'm in the hotel?'

'You'll have to take over his care. Though he don't eat much, he's been happy with the leftovers I've given him once a day.'

Yup, that would go some way to explaining why the dog was so skinny thought Cody. Out loud he said, 'Well I'm sure he appreciates your kindness and I'll be happy to relieve you of the burden from now on.' He moved toward the front door eager to go out and spend time with his dog.

'I've given him some water already this morning. There's a cafe down the street. You can get some breakfast for both of you there.'

'Thanks Belinda, I'll make sure I check it out. I might buy him some Kibbles, wouldn't want to carry on spoiling him with human food any longer.' Inwardly he winced at the thought of what slops Belinda might have given his dog, he was more than happy to share his food with his dog but until he was set up and able to prepare decent food he'd have to settle for giving the dog the more expensive option of store bought dried dog food.

'Is there a butcher I can buy some soup bones from? That'll give him something to chew on.'

'Now there's a good idea, I hadn't thought of that. I can tell you're a dog person. The butcher's on Main Street inside the grocery store, I expect he won't charge you much.'

That's what I was hoping, Cody thought.

He had his hand on the door when Belinda asked, 'If you're of a mind to hit the road again then you'll have to clear your room by three pm or we'll have to charge you for another night.'

'Oh I expect I'll be here one more night so I'll be back before three to pay up.' Thanking Belinda, he made his escape to the porch. The dog began thumping his tail against the floor boards as soon as he saw Cody step out the door. He rose in greeting tail wagging hard enough that he had to shift his feet to stay balanced.

'Hey boy!' Cody crouched down to meet the dog and rubbed him briskly behind the ears for a few seconds until the dog pressed forward so enthusiastically that Cody was knocked over onto his behind. Cody sat there making a fuss over his dog for a long time until eventually he calmed down and sat facing Cody. Cody shifted himself until his back came to rest on the wall and then reached behind him to pull out the block of wood from his pocket. The dog stretched out beside Cody, head still facing him, eyes closed, muzzle possessively on Cody's thigh. Cody rested his hand on the dog's head and relaxed, thinking through what he needed to do that day.

A job, I need to find a job and fast and also somewhere cheap to live, I can't afford to keep staying in this dump and besides I'd like my dog to be able to come indoors. Can't keep calling him 'the dog' though Cody thought.

'What should I call you boy?' The dog lifted his head and woofed softly, looking intently at Cody. An old Ford pickup truck rattled past them with *Jake's Hardware* stencilled on the side. Cody knew that legend had it that the Indians chose names based on the first thing they saw and while Cody didn't think he'd like a dog named truck, the name Jake would do nicely.

'Jake?' he said aloud, looking at his dog who woofed again thumping his tail before settling down to sleep.

Cody stayed on the porch with Jake for the better part of an hour, watching as the rain began to fall again and sensing the damp settle onto every fibre of his clothing. Eventually the downpour slowed to a drizzle. When it was no more than a mist Cody got up and stretched. Jake stood looking at Cody expectantly, tail in motion as usual.

'Ready for a walk Jake?' Jake huffed excitedly and they set off in the direction of the highway. Jake walked in time with Cody's steps without needing a leash, which made Cody think that someone had put time and effort into training him. Cody wondered what Jake's story was and half hoped he'd never find out, as the mystery was likely to only ever be solved if the owner came looking to claim Jake.

Cody and Jake wandered along the side of the highway for a while before Jake drifted off into the meadow that the highway bordered. Cody let him range ahead for a bit until he'd squatted and done his business, then called him back and they walked for a mile or so through the damp grass. The sun came out as the clouds slid away and the grass began to steam in the heat. Cody found a stick which he threw for Jake repeatedly until the stick was a soggy chewed mess and Cody could no longer bring himself to handle it. He wiped his hands on the sides of his jeans and called out to Jake who had suddenly shot off in pursuit of something. Jake vanished amongst the tall grass, occasionally leaping above the stalks to peer ahead before dropping back down barking loudly.

'What's he up to for Christ sake?' Cody said aloud to the field. 'Jake! Come here!' he bellowed, angry now.

Jake leapt one final time and his barking ceased. Cody could see by the direction that the grass stalks were bending that Jake was making his way back to him. Eventually Jake's face poked out with a gopher hanging from his mouth.

'Whosa clever boy Jake?' Cody filled with pride at his dog's resourcefulness. That must be how he'd survived on his own; by supplementing the scraps with whatever animal he could hunt. He allowed Jake to eat his kill before they headed back to town.

Chapter nine - Long hair 'n' all

There were a lot more people on Main Street now then there had been in the morning. Cody exchanged nods with a few of the men but no one smiled so he didn't either. Jake walked calmly at Cody's side pausing when Cody did and sitting down patiently whenever Cody came to a full stop. Cody was making his way slowly along Main Street hoping to see some 'help wanted' adverts. The majority of people he passed tipped their heads to avoid eye contact and hurried on without so much as a nod in response to his timid 'Hello'.

He thought he heard one old man mutter, 'Get a haircut you hippie.'

Cody lifted his hat and shoved his thin hair behind his ears wondering if he had imagined that comment or if its length really was offensive to these small town folk. *Perhaps I should tie it back before I ask for work? Tie it back with what? Does the length of my hair really matter in the grand scheme of things?* Clearly, in Lumen's Gate it seemed to. He settled for tucking it into the back of his collar.

Cody paused longingly outside the cafe absorbing the tantalising smell of frying bacon, fresh bread and coffee. *No! I've got to be sensible and save my money which means no served meals. I'll get some provisions from the store when I get Jake's bones instead*, Cody told himself. With that he forced himself to walk away from the delightful aromas towards the store. Cody told Jake to sit at the kerb side and then pushed open the store door. A bell above the door announced his entry and a woman's head peered at him curiously from the end of the aisle.

'Can I help you?' she asked.

'No thanks. I just need a few tins and some packaged goods. I'll have a look around myself.'

'Suit yerself.' She went back to dusting the items on the shelves.

Cody wandered around the few rows of tins and packaged food. He added some beef jerky, crackers, Spam, a small block of 'rat nip' style cheddar, strawberries and a jar of bread and butter pickles to his shopping basket before walking over to the woman who had stopped her busy-work and was now behind the front counter blatantly staring at him.

'You got family here?' she asked nosily as she totalled the items in his basket.

'Nope, staying at the hotel.'

'Why you here?'

'There's a hotel here, surely you've seen strangers in town before, what do they come to Lumen's Gate for?' Cody said, deliberately not answering her question.

'The only people who take a room at the Randall's hotel are the apple workers and the occasional travelling salesman. I know you ain't one of those as they eat at the cafe and move on early. Are you one of them dope smokers? What with your long hair 'n' all...'

'No! Cody was shocked she could think so though a growing sense of the limitations of rural community living was beginning to dawn on him. Folks had different ideas of what was acceptable out here he realised and his hair length seemed to be implying much more than the fact that he couldn't be bothered to cut his hair often enough to keep it short. 'I came out here looking for work at one of the orchards.'

She laughed. 'There's no apple work until harvest time, city boy.'

'Oh.' Cody said, crestfallen. *Shit*, he thought, *now what*?

'Want anything else?'

'No. Oh yes I do actually. You got any soup bones I could give my dog?'

''Spect so. Billy!' she hollered.

'You bellowed Darlene?' A short man in a stained white apron came out from a door at the back of the shop with big grin stretched across his face.

'Oh ain't you the funny one. ' Darlene said with an affectionate note to her voice. 'This fella's askin' for some soup bones for his dog.'

'Right y'are. Hang on a minute.' He moved behind the glass fronted rear counter, got busy with a large handful of fat marrow bones and brown butcher paper, emerging moments later with a lumpy string tied parcel. 'Kinda dog y'got?'

'Coon hound I think, name's Jake,' Cody said gesturing towards Jake who was sitting patiently at the kerb where Cody had left him.

'That looks like the dog that pitched up at the Randall's last week.'

'It is, I'm his new owner.'

'Where you hail from?' And, why are you here adopting stray dogs? Was what Cody suspected was Billy's unspoken question.

'I'm from Benchling originally. Came here yesterday looking for work. I was hoping to get hired on one of the orchards but it seems I'm a bit early in the season.'

'That y'are.'

'Well, I'll have to put my thinking cap on.' Cody paid for his goods, said goodbye and walked back to the hotel with Jake.

He sat with Jake around the back of the Randall's under the shade of a dogwood tree and had a picnic meal of Jerky, cheese, crackers and bread and butter pickles. Jake worked his way through all of the bones, stripping the shreds of meat off, then licking them clean before cracking some of them open to savour the marrow inside. Cody took his hat off and the room key from his pocket, and then stretched out enjoying the spring heat after the dampness of the rain that morning. The lack of sleep from the night before caught up with Cody and he dozed a while with his dog beside him, sheer contentment tracing a smile over his relaxed face. Chattering squirrels chased each other across the grass and up the tree causing Jake to bark and wake Cody. He dry scrubbed his face vigorously with his hands until he felt more awake. He wrapped up the leftover food and the bones that Jake hadn't cracked open, Cody set aside in the butcher paper to use tomorrow. *I'll sneak them in my room and hope they don't smell too much*, he decided. Cody turned the outside tap on and Jake stood there lapping direct from the stream of water. Cody scooped handfuls to drink from above Jake's head while he wondered what to do next. He knew couldn't afford to stay at the hotel for more than a few nights, job or no job.

After settling Jake on the porch Cody went into the hotel to pay for another night's stay. *Another period of time in which to hopefully find some work for room and board at least for Jake and me, if not for pay* Cody thought feeling saddened that his dream of rural friendliness hadn't come to fruition. Quite the opposite he realised, if anything the town's people seemed suspicious of his motives and altogether too eager for him to be on his way.

Chapter ten - Moving on

Cody stepped into the gloom of the hotel reception thinking, *I wish to Christ they'd put a light on*!

'Hello again.' Belinda's voice sounded disturbingly coquettish and Cody prayed it was only his imagination playing tricks on him, as the reality was too awful to contemplate with a woman old enough to be his mother.

'Hi, I've come to pay for another night, I'll be moving on tomorrow.'

'Darlene's already been on the blower to let me know she's decided that you're not mooching around here a looking for a place to grow some marijuana or make some hooch. I have to admit I'd been wondering but hadn't found a way to ask you outright.'

'Nope I'm a respectable person, and a broke one at that. I came here thinking I could pick up some work at one of the orchards but Darlene says they don't take people on in the spring.'

'That they don't, no need for help 'till harvest time. So where you gonna head for work now then?'

'Absolutely no idea. Still I've got 'till tomorrow to decide which way to walk when I hit the highway. In fact I might take Jake for another wander and see if I get inspired while I'm out there.'

'Plenty of beautiful country scenery to be had round here for hundreds of miles, everything from orchards, to forests, valleys, to mountains.'

'I'd like to rough it for a while actually, sleep under the stars, live off the land.' Cody blurted, surprising himself, as he had no idea where that idea had come from.

'Really? That must be a man thing 'cos Howard did exactly the same thing for a few years while I was married. He would drift back into town a few times a year and when my husband left, Howard settled down to help me with the business. I think that's why he's such a curmudgeon half the time, on account of his 'cabin fever' but even if I could cope without him, he's far too old for any of that malarkey now.'

'Well I'd sure be interested in hearing any tales he's got to tell.'

'I'll pass that on to him.'

Cody took out his wallet to pay Belinda, distracted by his thought and fumbling with his grip on his wallet. He slipped the money out noticing that he still had his bus ticket with Ellen's contact details on it. Well he'd only half intended to write to her and he sure wasn't going to write now only to tell her what a mess he'd made of his dreams of settling in a rural town. Perhaps he'd send her a note, tell her about Jake and his plans to live in the wilds until harvest time, make it sound like it was his choice rather than the only option. Which reminded him, he did need to send a letter to Lizzie to let her know he was fine. Cody knew she'd be sure to pass that info on to the rest of the family. Cody decided to leave out any mention of going to live rough when he wrote to Lizzie though, just in case he couldn't cope and had to bail out before harvest season and the promise of a paying job. Bail out to where? Cody knew that was the key question but he felt better by hedging his bets and choosing to believe that if he wanted to bail out of this crazy escapade then he could.

Jake stood; tail wagging vigorously, as soon as he saw Cody step onto the porch. 'Let's go for a walk boy.' Cody said slapping his thigh to call Jake to heel. Jake complied immediately, tail still wagging, feet padding up and down excitedly. Man and dog headed for the highway once again, the speed of their pace forcing a slight breeze to partly lift Cody's hair reminding him that the back of it was till tucked in his collar. Now that he knew what his next move was, Cody was no longer worried about having to make a good impression on the town people and ran his hand against the back of his neck freeing his hair from his collar. *Call me a hippie? Well I couldn't care less.* Cody's face settled into a picture of proud defiance as he strode determinedly towards tomorrow's promise of freedom, his dog happily keeping pace with him.

Cody paused when he got to the highway trying to decide, amongst other things, which direction he should set off towards tomorrow. He was certain that he could sleep under the stars until he learned how to build a shelter though he'd definitely need a sleeping bag. It was still cold at night this time of year even though the days were getting warmer. He stood still trying to think of what he else would need while Jake nosed excitedly in the deep ditch beside the road. *I need to write to Lizzie... in fact it would be a good idea to buy some paper, envelopes and stamps in case I want to write some more during the summer...though I'm not sure I will be anywhere near a post office.* Jake began wandering along the ditch, sloshing through the small amount of water at the bottom and Cody followed him simply because it was in the opposite direction of the way they'd gone that morning and he wanted to see what lay ahead. It didn't take long to clear the outskirts of Lumen's Gate and beyond lay orchards of fruit trees stretching as far as the horizon. Cody walked along the orchard boundary on the same side of the highway as Lumen's Gate taking in the view. He felt a sense of peace steal over him as he listened to the bird song and to Jake's contented snuffling punctuated with vigorous sneezes as he inspected the ground before him.

The shadows deepened as the afternoon moved towards evening and Cody began to retrace his steps. By the time the sky had become backlight by oranges and ambers instead of sun-brightened blue, Cody and Jake were most of the way back to the Randall's. All the shops were closed along Main Street except for the diner, which seemed somehow diminished and sunken into the evening shadows. *It looks like a chicken without its feathers*, Cody thought as he passed by resisting the urge to look in, lest the desire for a cooked meal should overwhelm his resolve to avoid spending money unnecessarily. *Best get used to some hunger pangs if I'm going to live off the land for a while*, Cody thought and experienced a frisson of pleasurable nerves.

'Not long now boy.' He said to Jake, who huffed in response.

Cody's boots crunched on some loose gravel scattered on the Randall's walk so he stopped and spent a minute moving it off the path with wide sweeps of his boots while he tried to phrase his opening lines to Howard Randall. He didn't want to inadvertently offend him again and even more importantly he desperately wanted to get as much information out of him on the subject of living rough. Settling Jake on the porch with some fresh water, Cody promised him some bones before he went to bed for the night and, after taking a deep breath, opened the door.

'Good evening to you.' Howard Randall shocked Cody by initiating the conversation.

'Nice to see you again.' Cody said sincerely to the looming bulk behind the counter.

'How's that dog of yours?' Howard's look was mildly challenging, as if daring Cody to tell him that he'd changed his mind about being a dog owner.

'He's great, I've named him Jake, he caught himself a gopher today!' Cody rattled off in a hurry to convince Howard of his worth as Jake's owner.

''Course he did, he's a coon hound, those dogs have been bred to hunt.' Howard grunted out a sigh and silence fell between him and Cody like a dead weight.

Shit, did I say something wrong? Cody wondered. Aloud he said, 'Belinda tells me you know a lot about wilderness survival.'

'Ayap. She told me you've a notion to rough it for a bit.'

'Seemed the sensible thing to do because my money won't see me though to harvest season otherwise.'

Howard grunted in response and began flicking through the register on the desk.

'Also I like the idea of making the most of what nature has to offer and just getting away from the peculiarities of other people for a while. At least when there's just Jake and then I won't have to worry about what others think of me.' Cody said wondering as he did so why he was baring his innermost thought to this dour old man.

'I felt much the same city boy, much the same, at your age. Still do in fact but it don't matter so much now that I'm older.'

'Was it hard?' Cody asked tentatively, scared of losing Howard's interest again.

'T'was and t'weren't. Depended on the time of year and how well prepared I'd gotten. T'was easier the more years I'd roughed it 'cos I knew what to do to get ready for the winters. Sure weren't keen on them to start with and used to come here at first until I'd built myself a small cabin that I used year round after that. Until I had to give it all up.' He finished bitterly.

'Belinda said you had to come home to help her out in the end.' Cody said but wisely left out the bit about Belinda thinking he'd have had to give it up anyway due to this advancing age.

'Yeah I did. She couldn't do it all on her own and it was time for me to grow up and take on my responsibility to the family business.' He went silent again, lost in thought.

Cody shifted his feet, unsure what to say, fighting to keep his many questions under control until he was sure it was okay to speak.

'Still got it all.' Howard blurted suddenly.

'Uh, still got what?' Cody asked in confusion.

'My outdoor gear. I've never had the heart to throw it away, guess I'd always hoped I'd use it again someday.'

'Oh. Well I can understand that. It'd be a waste to do otherwise.' Cody's heart had lurched with hope when he heard Howard say he still had all the gear. He'd been wondering where he'd be able to pick up what he needed as Lumen's Gate would be unlikely to keep much, if anything, in stock unless it related to rural farming needs, like the knife he had decided he would need.

'Yep, 'cept there's no hope I'll ever get to use it again now,' Howard said sadly. Cody stayed silent, his mind racing as he tried to think how to phrase his question.

'Say you'd have use for it though.' Howard's eyes had taken on a glint now. 'You cain't go living in the wilds without any gear. You ain't got any do yer?'

'No. I've spent most of today trying to think of what I'll need and where I can buy it from. I was hoping you'd be able to point me in the right direction.'

'I can do better than that, let me get my gear and while you look through it we'll have a chat about which of it might suit your needs best. Then we'll agree a price for it.'

'Great! Thanks! I need to feed Jake, is it okay to come back after that?'

'That might be a bit soon, I'm on duty here and as soon as I can get away for a time I'll grab my big rucksack and come find you.'

'If I'm not with Jake then I'll be in my room.' Cody said eagerly, a grin of anticipation on his face as he went to his room to get the leftover bones for Jake.

~ ~

Cody woke the next morning with a feeling of intense well being. He sat up and looked to his left where his wilderness survival kit was laid out. Howard had an amazing amount of gear packed tightly into the large rucksack which Cody had struggled to lift by himself though Howard seemed to handle it with ease. Towards the end of yesterday evening he had finally admitted to Cody that there was a knack to manoeuvring the load by using the weight of your body as a fulcrum instead of trying to lift it like you might try and lift a heavy box. Yesterday evening Cody had talked with Howard about which direction he planned to head in and Howard marked a few spots on the map where he reckoned Cody could go off road without trespassing on someone's land. The next step yesterday evening had been to go through Howard's gear and take out the items they were sure Cody wouldn't need. Howard told Cody a city boy like him would never manage any distance with the rucksack as full as it was even though he managed to master the swing lift technique to get it up onto his shoulders. After much deliberation Cody had ended up with one thick and one thin grey wool blanket, a pup tent, a kerosene fed lamp and fuel for it, a screw top enamel flask which he could use to carry water and cook in, matches in a plastic film canister (which Howard said would keep them dry), a steel wool pan scrubber (which Howard said was great for starting a fire if everything else was wet), a length of fishing line, a length of thin snare wire, a square of nylon netting, a length of waxed canvas, a survival book, a shovel without a handle and a large sheath knife with a clip point.

Howard had also listed some food items that Cody needed to take with him as emergency rations until he had his food gathering established. Cody had jotted them down to make sure he didn't forget anything; hard tuck rye bread (which Howard said would keep forever if it didn't get wet), molasses, whole meal flour, dried beans and pulses, jerked meat, vitamin C tablets, rolled oats, toilet paper, some kibble for Jake, soup broth cubes, instant coffee, a couple of tins of baked beans, a bag of salt and a box of dried milk. Before falling asleep last night Cody had practiced packing away his gear a few times, and the swing lift required to get it up onto his shoulders. He thought he had figured out the best fit combined with ease of access now though he knew he would have to add his few remaining items today before he left the hotel for good.

After buying the long life food on his list, Cody succumbed to his inner nag and spent some of his precious remaining money on an 'early bird' special of pancakes with extra syrup, back bacon and eggs cooked over-easy style. After wiping his plate clean with the last bit of pancake and enjoying a refill of his coffee, Cody escaped the curious stares of the other customers and went back to the Randall's to feed Jake a meal of kibble, which also would help to lighten the load that he'd need to carry. While Jake was eating, Cody packed the rest of the items in his rucksack including his treasures from home, emptied his bladder of the extra coffee and handed in his key to Belinda. He'd half dragged, half carried his rucksack to reception and rested it on the floor against the reception desk until he'd finished saying goodbye to Belinda and Howard before cheating by using the counter to steady his rucksack as he shrugged it on.

Howard laughed and said, 'I worry about you city boy.'

Cody laughed back and said 'You know I can get it on without help, you saw me do it last night, but if there's something to prop it on then it makes sense to take advantage of the help.'

'Yep. Waste not, want not. That's a good motto to remember now Cody.' Belinda said encouragingly.

'I call that rule number two!' Cody said and surprised himself by smiling as he pictured rule number two spinning gently until it twisted into a happier version of its old self.

''Spect you'll have some tales to tell next time we see you around.' Howard said hopefully. 'Now get on your way, the day's wasting.' With that Howard turned and made his way into the room behind reception, which Cody assumed led to his and Belinda's living quarters.

''Spect so.' Cody said to Howard's receding form. 'Bye now.' He said to Belinda.

'Bye. You take care now. Keep in touch.'

'Oh! That reminds me.' Cody fumbled in his front pocket until he'd pulled out the short letter he'd written to Lizzie and Charles last night and the slightly longer one to Ellen. 'Need to mail these on my way out of town.'

He had decided to make light of the fact that there was no work till harvest time and much of the fact that he was going to spend the summer 'having fun in the wilderness boy scout style'. Cody had mentioned the advice Howard had given him and the survival equipment he'd bought off him. He had told them about Jake in great detail to fill the empty space on the paper and finished by promising to write more in the autumn but planned to write one or two more before then to Ellen if all was going well enough for him to have something to tell her which wouldn't do any damage to his ego.

Cody stood on the hotel porch for a few moments, adjusting to the weight of the rucksack before walking down the steps with Jake to give him a big drink of water. Cody then said a quiet good bye to all that he disliked about modern civilisation and began walking towards the highway with his dog keeping pace by his side. He passed the general store in a world of his own but Darlene was bored with dusting the shelves and sat waiting for something interesting to happen outside the window. She rapped on the window as he passed and Cody stopped, grinned at her and turned back to post Lizzie and Ellen's letters.

'Thought I'd seen the last of you when you bought your groceries this morning.' Darleen said brightly. 'I saw you go past just now and the look on your face made me think of how my Billy had looked when I first fell in love with him so many years ago.'

'Just need to post these letters,' Cody explained, wanting to change the subject.

'Billy!' Darlene bellowed, then in a quieter voice to Cody, 'He'll be pleased to know you've come back in, he wanted a chance to say goodbye.'

Billy's head poked round the corner of the back room. 'Ah, hello there. On your way are you?'

'Yup.' Cody shifted his shoulders up, moving the rucksack on his back. He hadn't wanted to take it off when he came in the store just in case he found it difficult to shrug it on outside the store. He'd had enough of hearing the 'city boy' term thrown in his direction without wanting to give anyone good reason to think it.

'Thought that coon hound of yours could do with some bones. No charge to you, come back and tell me some tales of your time out in the woods in trade this winter.'

'Deal.' Cody turned round so Darlene could tie the bones in their plastic bag onto the bottom outside of his rucksack.

'There, that'll do nicely till you want it for your dog later.' Darlene patted Cody's rucksack, satisfied with her handiwork.

The mist was rising off the meadows on either side as the sun rose and warmed all that it shone down on including Cody. Filled with a sense of anticipation and hope about what the future had in store for him for the first time in years, he strode confidently along the gravel that lined the side of the road, each step moving him closer to his new life.

Chapter eleven - Roughing it

Cody walked for miles that first morning, off road when he could and along the road when he had to. The scenery changed more frequently than he had expected after the few apple orchards outside Lumen's Gate disappeared giving way to fields full of young corn, potatoes and tomato plants. The beauty of the orchards full of fruit trees in full blossom was a sight that Cody tried to fix permanently in his mind. He wanted to keep that memory tucked away safely where he could bring it out like a treasured photograph to rest his mind on at will. Jake alternated between ranging ahead and bounding back to Cody full of the enthusiasm of a very happy dog. Cody stopped for lunch at the edge of a meadow, finishing the leftovers from yesterday's picnic outside the hotel while Jake savoured a couple of bones. Afterwards Cody stretched out with his head on his rucksack, face shaded by his hat, Jake at his side and slept for a while in the warmth of the afternoon.

A car honked its horn as it went past some time later, waking Cody. He nudged Jake into wakefulness who sprang into action, shaking off sleep with the speed of a small child. Cody stretched and drank water from his canteen while Jake lapped noisily at the water in the bottom of the roadside ditch. Consulting the map, Cody thought of the miles ahead and deliberated hitchhiking a ways along the route he had planned. A few minutes of mental wrestling later, he decided that hitchhiking went against his concept of roughing it and started walking again.

Just keep putting one foot in front of the other he told himself *and it will soon be time to set up camp for the night*. He spent time throwing a stick for Jake, laughing as his dog leapt into the air twisting his body from side to side like a flopping fish as he tried to pluck the stick out of the air. Cody continued to walk off road where he could which became impossible whenever the meadows turned to water laden marshlands or fell away into sharp drops. At these points Cody had to backtrack towards the road, always keeping the forest he could see in the distance to his left. Eventually, as the late afternoon sky deepened from the watery spring blues into evening hues of orange and umber, Cody decided to set up camp for the night. He calculated that he'd walked between fifteen and twenty miles that day and was grateful that he would reach his new home by tomorrow evening at the latest. At least he should do so according to the route that Howard had shown him on the map as long as he set out early enough the next morning. He moved deeper into the meadow he had been walking through, aiming for a distant cluster of trees. He pitched his tent close by the trees and scratched a wide circle of bare soil on which to build his fire. Gathering firewood quickly he managed to get his fire lit just as dusk fell. Jake kept close to him, nearly tripping Cody up on a few occasions as he foraged for firewood and Cody eventually made Jake sit by the tent until he had finished his tasks, in order to keep them both accident free. In the growing darkness, stomach growling, Cody heated a tin of beans. He had something to eat late afternoon but the walking had used up that food long ago and he knew that the beans wouldn't be enough. That afternoon he had discovered that Darlene had secretly added a few potatoes, a bag of onions, a bag of salty potato sticks and a block of butter to the bag which had Jake's meaty bones in it. He loved her at that moment of discovery and had eaten half the bag of potato sticks mid afternoon. Keeping one potato, Cody had suspended the rest of the food from a high tree branch away from his campsite before he had gathered the last of his firewood. Now Cody placed the potato in the coals to roast and ate his beans thinking they tasted better than anything he'd eaten in a long time. He decided that it must be all the fresh air he had today that had sharpened his taste buds. Jake ate a double handful of the dried dog food and then contently licked and crunched a soup bone. Cody had found clean fast running water that afternoon and had filled his canteen with it. He savoured a coffee while he waited for his potato to cook, having drunk his fill of plain water during the day. *I could get tired of having just water day after day pretty darn quick, still it's better than having no water I guess, best not complain lest I jinx myself*, he thought. He dug the potato out of the coals and lifted it onto his plate, split it open and sprinkled it with salt before smearing butter all over the soft insides with his knife.

He savoured the creamy potato flesh, aware he was making involuntary 'ummmm'ing noises, and glad that no one besides Jake was there to hear him. Cody gave the ash-dusted jacket to Jake who wolfed it down with a couple shakes of his head. Cody and Jake walked companionably a ways away from their camp, though not out of reach of the glow of the camp fire, and did their nightly toileting business before Cody banked the camp fire. Crawling into the tent to sleep, he rolled himself up in his blankets, leaving Jake outside cuddled up to the rucksack. With the sudden lack of things with which to occupy his mind his thoughts were accosted by a deluge of random and not entirely welcome thoughts. Brushing aside the hurt that came in on the wake of his mother's unexplained departure, his father's refusal to acknowledge that Cody was a more than just a boy and Lizzie's complacent acceptance of it all; Cody focused on the soft fuzz that came over him everywhere except his groin which leapt into urgent focus whenever he indulged himself with thoughts of the sight and smell of Ellen. Once he had relieved himself of that pressure, Cody was relaxed enough in body and mind to drift off to sleep.

  He slept intermittently during the night, frequently waking to puzzle at individual noises from outside his tent. He had grown accustomed to nightlife of a human variety in the city but he'd no idea that it could be so busy or loud at night in the great outdoors. Some sounds like owls and bats were easily identifiable, other noises enigmatic to the extreme. At one point he had to resort to lighting his lantern in order to identify what the scratching was outside the tent, it wasn't bothering Jake which meant that there was no immediate harm about to befall them, but threat or no threat, until Cody knew what was making the noise he couldn't get to sleep. The culprits were stag beetles. Cody shook his head and, knowing there was no way he could silence them, extinguished his light and went to work on falling back asleep. It wasn't until he relaxed enough to begin drifting towards sleep again that he worked up the strength to question his motives for moving further and further away from home. The answer came in the form of rule number one. *Avoidance tactic* he told his near dream self truthfully, *that's all you're doing*.

Cody woke slowly the next morning with the weight of sad assurance that as long as he kept himself unreachable then he could fool himself into thinking that everything he loved and relied on was still at home. The thought that his mother may have been nudging him from the nest by leaving herself fluttered across his mind and he fiercely swept it aside before the truth of it could hurt him. *I stayed at home long after I wanted to leave in order to protect my mother from my father* he told himself firmly, and accepted no more arguments from the lingering fragments of his dream self.

He emerged from the tent on all fours only to be almost knocked over as he was greeted joyously by Jake.

'Just you and me boy, huh?' Cody patted him before he stood and stretched the night from his muscles.

Jake leaped at him, muzzling his boots and wanting to play. It was at moments like these that he became certain Jake was very young; probably still mostly a puppy, even though his mid thigh level height implied otherwise. Once again Cody wondered how Jake had come to end up on the Randall's porch. Cody sighed, habitually discontent with mornings, and then realised that he was grateful for Jake's effervescent, mood lifting personality. This morning, and hopefully many others, was a good one that felt right and smelled of freedom.

  Cody and Jake drank water and then ate oatmeal with milk powder and water for breakfast, though Cody added some kibble to bulk out Jake's portion. Jake licked his dish clean but Cody decided not to wash his pot and utensils out until he found some fresh water, as the level in his canteen was low enough to begin conserving it where possible now. He knew there was a small river running parallel to him but according to the map it was too far away at the moment so he was aiming to angle towards it over several hours of hiking and set up camp once he had found a nice place along the riverbank. He packed up his camp, cursing his tent, which was apparently reluctant to fit back into the straps under the rucksack as easily as it had when Howard had forced it into a diminutive roll. Cody finally shaped it into a more acceptable size and squashed it mostly inside its canvas bag, pulling the straps of the rucksack over the tent and tying it firmly in place. He tied his lantern and pot alongside the bag with his goods from the store, kicked ample soil over the smouldering embers of his camp fire and set off with Jake bounding ahead and then back like a canine boomerang.

Chapter twelve - Sweet River Camp

They walked seemingly endless miles, and as they did the sun warmed the air, gently at first before growing uncomfortably hot. Cody was glad they had set out early because they had managed to cover many miles in the cool of the morning. Early afternoon they stopped for a rest and lunch under the shade of a blossom covered gnarled crab apple tree growing randomly on an outcropping of rocks. Cody resisted the urge to take his boots off and air his hot feet because he feared he would not be able to force them on again after lunch. Instead, he used his hat to flap waves of air towards his sweaty face and throat and tried to ignore the persistent throb emanating from his overworked feet. There wasn't much moving in the still of the afternoon except for the persistent flies, which followed them like their own mini black cloud. *Be nice if they threw some shade on us and that's a fact*, Cody thought as he swatted at one who had moved in to sample the sweat still drying on his brow. Jake lay at his side, panting, his tongue dripping precious fluid onto the dry rocks. Cody was glad that he'd seen Jake drinking from a shallow pond earlier otherwise he would be worried about Jake dehydrating from all the exercise in the unseasonable heat. He switched from wafting air at his own face and began directing it towards Jake, laughing as the warm breeze made Jake's ears twitch until Jake rolled onto his side and pawed at Cody's leg as if to say 'alright, enough already'. Jake and Cody dozed for a while after lunch before pressing on towards what Cody thought was to be their new home.

Fat bees bumbled their way around flower heads and the crickets thundered their way through their concerts, always finishing with the same crescendo, which then crashed into an absolute but momentary silence, before their music began once again to spiral up through the same gleeful composition which serenaded Cody and Jake along this portion of their travels. They didn't have to walk for long that afternoon before they could hear the river tumbling and splashing its way downstream. Cody headed directly for it, climbed down the bank and turned to face upstream as he drank copiously from his cupped hands, tightening his leg muscles against the strong flow of the water. He could understand why it had been named Sweet River, the water tasted pure and delicious. Jake trundled downstream stopping to nose around in the shallows at the river edge and drink noisily from time to time as if searching for the perfect flavour. Cody sat in the shade of a willow on the bank, boots wet around the bottom seams and watched Jake, feeling drowsy and content despite his aching feet. When Jake wandered back Cody stood and shrugged the rucksack back on, wincing at the feel of the blisters on his heels and side of his foot as he moved forward again. Cody comforted himself with the thought that he could go barefoot for a whole week if he chose to do so once he reached the unseen spot that he had already named Sweet River Camp.

By late afternoon Cody and Jake had reached the spot he had already begun to think of as home, one of the places Howard had marked off on the map as being owner free and therefore carrying little risk of trespass. He pitched his tent on the pebbled shore that ran into the wide stream of crystal clear river water. As the sun began to dip in the sky, mosquitoes rose on the cloud of damp that had been held at bay all day. Cody hadn't thought to buy any citronella oil or any other kind of mosquito repellent and was rapidly beginning to regret this oversight, first flies and now mozzies. Already he could tell that life here without insect repellent would be a grim torture. He pulled moss and lichen to dry overnight and use as future fire starter, slapping at the minuscule winged instruments of torture all the while. For his fire tonight, Cody planned to use some of the steel wool he had bought at the store, like he had done the night before. The rest he promised himself that he would save for emergencies. Cody grinned as the refashioned rule two: waste not, want not popped into his head. He had made a pact with himself to live off the land as much as possible, for as long as he needed to, although setting up some sort of a durable homestead was on his mental 'to do before winter' list. He quickly gathered enough firewood to last him well into the next day and after clearing a patch of earth a safe distance from his tent, Cody brought his campfire to life with ease.

Howard had explained the basics of lighting a camp fire: lots of room underneath to let the oxygen in and nice dry tinder to set the spark off into, kindling on top of the tinder, then very dry sticks of increasing girths stacked on top of the kindling building them on top of each other, working from tepee to box style. Cody had found these instructions easier to follow than he had originally thought possible. Blowing on the small flame helped to force it past the kindling stage and the sticks soon caught alight. When it was burning strongly Cody added a couple of large logs so that they could burn down into cooking coals by suppertime. Removing his boots he breathed a sigh of relief then examined his feet with trepidation but after close inspection he was happy to see they didn't look as bad as they felt. Barefoot, he made several trips back and forth, eventually gathering enough large stones from the riverbed to form a wide ring around his campfire pit before wandering back over to the river edge to contemplate his chances of catching a fresh meal.

As he stood on the pebbles which lined the water's margin trying to decide whether it would be best to try and catch a fish with his net or line, he noticed mud still eddying around the areas where he had recently removed stones and realised this might be enough to keep the buzzing, biting, nightmares at bay. He scooped handfuls of mud onto a large log, which jutted conveniently out of the shrubbery at the river's edge, shuddering at the sensation of it squelching through his fingers. A mental image of a leech sent him rushing into the water to frantically wash the remnants of the mud off his hands. Cody dithered once more considering how best to try and catch his supper. Another bite on the back of his wet hand, this time from a horse fly, forced him overcome his leech repulsion. Cody first smeared the mud on the palms of his hands to check for wriggling leeches and then spread it thinly over his exposed skin. Cody momentarily delighted in the blessed relief the mud provided and then spent the next several minutes wriggling his nose against the itch and trying not to scratch the mud off as it pulled his skin while it dried.

  Cody spent the next few days testing out and developing the new skills he needed to survive off the land. Catching fish in a net proved quite simple once he had found a good hiding spot on the bank and perfected the swooping motion needed to net the thrashing meal. Cody devised a spit of sorts over his campfire from two forked sticks. He ran an almost straight stick lengthways through the gutted fish and roasted them to perfection several days in a row, eating his fill a few times a day until he tired of the taste. Jake's soup bones were long gone, and although he supplemented small amount of kibble with whatever rodent he was able to catch, he was more than happy to eat fish when Cody offered. He too preferred his fish cooked though he would eat it raw when he tired of waiting for Cody to cook it. Cody wanted to begin to dry fish strips into jerky to set aside for winter but knew he'd have to make some kind of storage container to hold the fish until he wanted to eat it. There were two main problematic issues with this idea that he could think of; how to keep it dry and how to keep it from appealing to bears or any other hungry predators. Although he hadn't seen any so far he knew that mating and cub seasons would be a risky time.

  After consulting his survival book and a couple of days' experimentation Cody made an irregular shaped vessel from birch bark. As advised by the survival book, he was careful to keep the tree alive by using only the pale outer layer and leaving the dark brown inner bark attached to the tree. He stitched the container together with split, flattened spruce roots, which he pushed through small holes he'd made with his knife. Cody spread heated spruce pitch over the seams to seal them and decided that the smell might actually be just the thing to keep interested animals away. He jotted a note in his book to remind himself to cover the filled container with the pungent pitch. His heightened awareness of pungent smells got him to thinking about Jake's bowel movements. He realised that he might have found a use for them at last and made another note to collect Jake's stools and stack them over the spot where he planned to bury his containers filled with dried meat in rock lined cache. Cody spent several days busily alternating between making containers, catching fish, slicing the fillets into thin strips, dusting them with salt and drying them suspended way above the fire on a rack he'd made of woven saplings which he soaked overnight before use each day in order to prevent it burning. Above all he made sure that he kept himself too busy to think of anything but the tasks before him. There was ample time to ponder the challenges of his previous life each evening after the sun had sunk below the horizon, and all too often Ellen was his both his last and first waking thought.

He had begun writing a paragraph or two each morning summarising what he had done or discovered the previous day and had formed a vague plan to tuck it into an envelope one day before winter and head off in search of a car to flag down and ask if they would be willing to take the stamped envelope which was addressed to

Ellen to the nearest post office. He told himself that she would be pleased to know he had thought to take the time to write her each day even if the writing was no more than the roughing it equivalent of small talk.

The fish shrunk a lot during the drying process and Cody managed to smoke what he thought was sufficient to see him through a good part of the winter. He had decided to look upon this first year as a learning process, and told himself he could always pack up and head back to civilisation if he needed to though he knew that he didn't relish the idea of making that hike back if he ran out of food once winter was well and truly set in. Once his fish jerky was ready he transferred it into his containers, covering each one completely with pitch once the lid was secured on. Some distance away from his camp Cody dug a few four-foot deep pits and lined them with the small stones he had collected from along the river and allowed to dry before use. He placed the containers in their pits and covered them with the stones and then with soil. On top of the soil he piled more stones, which he then topped with Jake's excrement. The piles didn't look pretty and he was fairly certain that they would remain unappealing to carnivores long enough to allow him and Jake to eat the contents during the food scarce winter months to come. Cody decided that although he would be grateful for whatever he could get in the winter, he was currently thoroughly fed up with fish and was craving fresh meat, vegetables and fruit.

His survival guide had a chapter on how to make snares and Cody had set about trying to make a working hoop snare the day he and Jake found the rabbit burrow. Jake was dancing around in excitement, repeatedly standing up on his hind legs and then dropping with an audible blow onto his front paws, sniffing at the numerous entrances and exits until Cody called him to heel so he could concentrate. He spent a lot of time studying the rabbit trails to see where the beat was, which the book described as the place where the rabbits repeatedly placed their feet as they ran along their trails. He then pushed the ends of the legs of his hoop snare onto either side of the rabbit run with the loop of the snare poised at setting height over a 'beat' mark. He checked and readjusted his snares every few hours until he found a trapped rabbit the next day. Cody felt horrified when he realised that the soft furred animal was still alive. Somehow the rabbit's distress bothered him much more than the fish thrashing about when they were in their death throes in his fishing net.

'Fartknocker!' Stress made Cody slip back into the comfort of a favoured curse he'd used as a boy. Taking a deep breath and shushing Jake who was whimpering with excitement, he picked up the rabbit by the hind legs until it was suspended just above the ground and then karate chopped it on the back of its neck twice until it hung limply from his hand.

'Good thing I'd read what to do in the book, eh boy?' Cody said nervously to Jake as he set about freeing the dead rabbit from the snare wire.

Jake stood very still, eyes fixed on the soft crumpled bundle that lay on the ground before him and whined plaintively.

'No Jakey! You don't get to eat a whole one to yourself unless you caught it or I manage to snare a few at a time.' Cody was aware that he was talking to Jake more frequently now and in a conversational tone rather than a 'master bidding his dog' tone.

Cody was missing human conversation more than he had expected. It seemed the old adage – you don't know what you've got till it is gone – was true in more ways than one. Just a few weeks ago he had been desperate to get away from all things to do with civilised living and now, although he didn't miss the majority of it, he sure longed to be able to chat with someone who could challenge his well thought out philosophical musings with more than a variable toned bark and occasional look of utter disdain. Cody tutted at himself and reset the snare before walking back to camp, keeping well away from the rest of the snares he'd set on the trail. They'd been empty when he checked them earlier and he knew that he couldn't face checking them again at the moment. Cody hung the rabbit from a branch that was at his chest height and began skinning it. He halved the rabbit carcass and placed it in a pot of water, along with a garlic bulb that he'd dug up and beans that he'd cooked earlier, and left the ingredients to stew together while he buried the skin and entrails well away from his living area.

Over the past couple of weeks while wandering around the land he considered his territory, with Jake laying down his scent every few feet to make it officially his, Cody had found several useful plants. One of them was a cluster of cattails growing in a small marsh, and he was in the process of digging up and drying these to use as a starch during the winter. Cody had also made note of where the most prolific patches of burdock were, as he wanted to try drying the peeled roots of these plants as well. He'd also discovered a large patch of about three-dozen wild strawberry plants with plentiful berries to be; some still tiny and green and others already turning white, which meant the pink to red would follow soon. He made a note of the spot so that he could come back in a week to check their progress, he wanted to time it right in order to harvest the berries before the birds and insects got at them.

  He knew that the Indians called the full moon in June the 'strawberry moon' and by the looks of those little white berries he guessed that this was when the first of his strawberries would be ready for harvest. Water was plentiful and it hadn't upset his stomach yet so he assumed it was as clean as it looked. Cody no longer feared a leech encounter and had continued to use the mud as a mosquito repellent, washing it off in the mornings and reapplying it in the late afternoon. His sleeping bag was covered in the stuff and Cody had taken to brushing it off in the mornings but knew he would have to wash it long before winter because it would take a few days to dry which meant sleeping without it while it dried. For now he chose to live with the stained sleeping bag.

Chapter thirteen – Bear

One morning Cody was vigorously scrubbing himself clean in the cool river water downstream from his camp when he heard Jake growl low in his throat as he rose to a stiff legged stance which was swiftly followed by a human shout.

'Hi over there! Coming towards you! Name's Bear.'

Cody startled and looked around, trying to cover his private parts as best he could with his hands, while stumbling out of the water and onto the pebbled shore.

The man who called himself Bear stood on the other side of the river from Cody's living area, knee deep in meadow grass, holding onto the barrel of an over-and- under shotgun which had been broken open at the breach, stock hooked over his shoulder.

Cody shushed Jake and told him to lie down, and the dog complied reluctantly. The man was dressed in jeans and boots and wore a leather vest over his long sleeved tee shirt. His hair, a uniform grey, hung to his shoulders. Cody decided that the name Bear was apt because the man was of more than average height and his bulk, which looked suspiciously muscular under the outer layer of fat, made him lumber in a 'bear-ish' fashion as he made his way along the river to where Cody had set up camp. He paused while still a short distance away until Cody had forced his wet limbs into his clothing.

'Hello. Sorry about being in the buff, didn't expect to see anyone round these parts…' Cody blustered, embarrassed.

'Not a problem, a man's got to keep his'self clean.'

'Erm…' Cody was at loss for words, unsure of the etiquette expected in this situation. He had no claim on this land but after living here for the past four weeks it already felt like home and this mans' uninvited presence almost felt like trespass.

'Coffee?' he said in an attempt to take control and mark this as his territory.

'Don't mind if I do.' Bear took his boots off, rolled up his jeans and made his way through the water to the side where Cody's camp was set up.

Cody made Jake lie down beside the tent and then busied himself with stoking up the fire. After hanging the pan full of water off an angled stick to boil in the heat, he gestured toward a couple of logs placed by the fire and said, 'Have a seat.'

Bear sat and the log sunk a ways into pine needled covered ground. Cody took a seat on the log opposite Bear's and called Jake over to sit in front of him. Neither of them spoke for a while. Jake bristled and gave an occasional half growl. Cody didn't bother to shush him anymore as he sensed Jake had himself under control and the growls were posturing more than an overt threat.

'He's a fine looking dog.' Bear remarked.

'Yup, and fair enough like a furry body guard.' Cody said. He handed Bear a mug of coffee and flinched as Bear reached for it with blood-stained nails. Bear saw him flinch, looked down at his hands and muttered 'Gah!' in an undertone.

'Rabbit blood. I hid them in a hurry when I heard your splashin'. Thought you might be a wild critter. Got my shotgun with me just in case but needed my hands free to use it and the rabbits in one piece when I'm ready to head home. Forgot to wash my hands.' He made his way to the river and cleaned his hands before coming back to drink his coffee in a couple of gulps.

'Steel lined mouth?' Cody was using a small birch bark bowl for his coffee and it was still half full as he offered, then poured, Bear a refill from the pot.

Bear laughed. 'Yup, got used to drinking it in a hurry. So...seems we've got a mutual interest.'

Cody frowned, 'What do you mean?'

'This.' Bear gestured to Cody's camp area. 'You're on my land.'

Cody did his best to hide his disappointment. 'I was led to believe this land wasn't owned by anyone.'

'Yup, p'raps so but it sure is. I came good on the lottery 'bout fifteen years ago and bought five hectares. Planted myself some cherry and apple trees on two of them over that way, and got a hundred head of livestock further back.' Bear gestured towards the way he'd come. 'I've left the other three, this land here, mostly wild for paying hunting parties during the November to December season. If you'd hiked further afield you would eventually have reached the hunting cabins on the edge of my orchard.'

'Oh. I don't know what to say except I'm sorry for trespassing. If you could give me until tomorrow morning to clear off I'd sure appreciate it.'

'No need to rush off. I'm happy to let you stay put here 'till hunting season makes it too risky.' He smiled then added, 'For a price.'

'I've got next to no cash on me, no more than pin money.' Cody's leftover money wasn't a fortune but is was his safety net in case he couldn't find a job straight away when he decided it was time to look for one. Remember rule number one: never lie, he took a deep breath and added, 'Truth is I do have money but would prefer to save it. So, I'll clear off your land by this time tomo...'

Bear interrupted, 'Happy to trade in kind. Got anything you can offer?'

Cody felt sick. He'd heard of men like Bear. 'Sick, perverts, homos or faggots' his dad called them. He felt the hairs on his arms bristle. Unlike his dad Cody had nothing against men who preferred dalliances with their own gender, but it was of no interest to him as a man.

'Oh shit! Erm, hey Bear? No offence intended, big man, but I guess I should make it clear that I don't bat for the other side!' Cody said, shocked beyond belief. Going by outward appearances he would have put his money on Bear being a biker with a predilection for 'Motorcycle Mommas'. He glanced round wondering if he and Jake could indeed make an escape should the seemingly benign Bear decide to take from him, whatever thing he was after. He noticed Bear was laughing silently, mouth wide, looking at the sky, tears streaming from his eyes. *Oh fuck* thought Cody. *No one sane laughs like that; I'm stuck here with a lunatic!* 'Why's that funny?' Cody demanded, a petulant edge to his question.

'I guess I should have explained more clearly what I meant.'

'Oh?' Cody was cautiously hopeful that Bear might want something he was willing to provide. *Maybe he needs some help at the orchard*; Cody thought to himself, *that, I'm willing to do!*

'For example, what have you been eating since you've been here?'

'Fish and dried beans mostly. I've tried to set up rabbit snares but other than one on the first day I've not caught any more.'

'So, I quite like fish but don't have the patience to catch any. You catch a few for me on a weekly basis and I'll call it quits. I'll make a point of driving out here every seven days to collect them from you.'

'I can do that.' Cody said earnestly. 'Do you want them fresh or smoked?'

'Two fresh and one smoked will do me nicely.'

The two men stood and shook hands. Then Jake sniffed Bear's hand which smelled agreeably of fresh rabbit overlaid with coffee and the scent of Cody. He wagged his tail limply a few times, more relaxed around Bear now but still guarded.

'You want me to look at your trap lines?' Bear offered.

'That would be great thanks.' Cody walked Bear to where he'd set his hoop snares.

'The solution is this,' Bear squatted and held his hand, palm down, about six and a half inches above the ground, 'your snare needs to be set at this height, you had it too high, the rabbits have been hopping safely underneath it.

'Shit, I'm an idiot!'

'I reckon you've done all right for having made working snares after reading how to in a book. And, having set it too high isn't necessarily a bad thing because it will have given them time to get used to the smell.'

Cody and Bear moved along the trap line resetting the snare heights.

'I don't 'spect you'll have much of a surplus of rabbit meant with Jake around, but if you do then they dry well. Just split them in half and smoke them till dry, bones and all. Works a treat though you'll need an iron drum for that kind of smoking or it'll take too long.'

'I don't have anything like that.'

'Thought not. Well see how you get on and if you've a need for one I can always drive one through to you.'

Bear said his goodbyes to both Cody and Jake and slowly ambled off into the distance of the meadow.

Chapter fourteen - Berry confectionery

In July there were plenty of ripe huckleberries, which added a nice flavour to both his rapidly dwindling supply of morning oats and the now plentiful meat supply. Cody had overcome his aversion to despatching the rabbits that had been caught but not killed by his snares. He had eaten less than his fill of the succulently perfumed strawberries. Jake had sampled a few, begged for more and sulked when Cody refused. Cody had to force himself to dry the rest to be enjoyed as a sweet treat in the winter as it was so Jake was out of luck despite his best efforts to convince Cody otherwise through begging and sulking. Cody struggled to get the strawberries completely dry; they remained slightly sticky no matter how long he left them in the sun. They tasted like confectionery and Cody was certain there was a market for unusual tastes like those berries. However, figuring out how to go about introducing his concept to the general public was a subject he couldn't even begin getting his head around. He made it as far as wondering if Billy and Darlene would be interested in selling them in their store, stumbled on the question of how to package them for sale and how to get them there and gave up on the whole idea completely.

P'raps I'll spend some time finding solutions to these things in the winter, Cody thought, *p'raps not*.

Bear had been as good as his word and had come by a week after he'd first met Cody, driving a battered looking red Ford pickup truck. He'd collected his fish and dropped off a cleaned out steel barrel into which he had cut a hole and fashioned a door from the steel he had removed. Bear had shown Cody how to use it to smoke the rabbit meat to perfection. Cody had used the relatively cool top of the barrel to dry the strawberries and was now contemplating how he might best preserve some of the surplus of blackberries that were hanging heavily from the brambles. They hadn't dried well when he had tried the same method as the strawberries. He had picked blackberries till his fingers were stained purple from the perfumed juice that burst from the soft, sun warmed fruit. They filled the picking basket with the scent of summer in a way that defied description. Jake had developed a taste for the berries too and, unable to get them off the brambles himself, he would eagerly wait and watch Cody's every movement while he was collecting blackberries so as not to miss any that Cody threw his way. *It never occurred to me that dogs would like fruit and vegetables*, Cody thought each time Jake's appetite demanded a new flavour. *It'd be a shame to let them go to waste as wasp food* Cody thought anxiously, once again fretting over how best to preserve them for winter despite the fact that Bear had made it clear that it wouldn't be safe for him to stay where he was. He had been in survival mode for the past couple of months and was now in the habit of putting aside everything he could in the hopes that he would be able to survive the winter ahead.

Thread! I run thread through the berries and hang them to dry in the tent! Cody grinned with relief, once he had figured out how to hang the berries in his tent then he could go about his other chores without having to worry about keeping the birds and insects from eating them.

'The more food, the better,' he muttered. Jake woofed softly in response.

He wasn't sure what would happen during hunting season and was hoping Bear would say that he would tell the hunters that his living area was off limits though he hadn't mentioned this to Bear yet. Cody wasn't convinced that he could survive the winter living in his tent or any shelter he built for himself even though the survival manual had a couple of ones they recommended. He had half a mind to ask Bear if he could work for him come winter time but hadn't yet as doing so seemed to make a mockery of all the food he was setting aside at the moment.

Why am I doing all this work if I'm just going to go live indoors and earn enough money to buy my food? That was a question Cody kept asking himself and as he hadn't come up with an answer, he hadn't been willing to discuss anything in relation to that with Bear.

He had been looking forward to his conversations with Bear about many other things though. It was now a routine for Bear to stay on and have a meal and a chat about various random topics with Cody each time he collected his fish. Bear usually brought something with him to contribute to the meal; Cody was particularly fond of the sourdough loaves Bear made. Cody hadn't figured out how to make bread but he enjoyed thinking up new recipes to make with the fresh ingredients he was able to gather. The survival book he'd bought off Howard had been most useful in that respect. Today he was going to roast a couple of big fish with some steamed lamb's quarter weed, garlic leaf and violet flowers. He'd also chanced upon a large patch of cow peas which he'd eaten both fresh and dried. He'd ground the dried ones down into a coarse powder which he mixed into a paste and fried thin. Once he'd worked out how to peel it off the pan all in one piece, it resembled a green tortilla and made a handy catch all for bits of meat and fish.

'Makes a nice change from yeasty bread.' Bear mumbled around his last mouthful of the meal.

'That's one of the things I miss the most, that and...' Cody felt his face flush as Bear looked at him questioningly.

'Family?'

Eyes fixed on the ground Cody shook then nodded his head. 'Mixed bag, miss some of my family sure, but mostly I'm missing a gal I met on the bus out here.'

'A looker, is she?'

'Yes and...more.' Cody struggled to find words to explain that which he hadn't figured out himself.

'Missed opportunities, they can play on a man's mind.' Bear dug a boot heel into the ground and frowned.

'You sound like you know what you're talkin' 'bout.'

'Yes well, I've been around lot of years now. Man's bound to make a mistake or two in life.' Bear's face matched the sheepish tone of his voice.

'I wonder,' Cody began then hesitated.

'So do I!'

They both laughed and a comfortable silence drifted between them for a while until Bear stood up and held out his hand, 'Anything you want me to bring next time?'

'Nothing in particular but would you mind posting a couple letters for me next time you go into town?'

'Won't be for a few weeks but happy to do that for you then.'

Cody gave Bear the bulging envelope filled with his pages of writing to Ellen, a thin one addressed to Lizzie containing a letter for her and Sandy to share, and money for the stamps.

Just over a month later Bear brought back two letters for Cody.

Astonished, Cody said 'But how does anyone know where to find me?'

Bear made the same noise then said 'I, uh, took the liberty of putting my address as the return in case they went astray. I hope I haven't caused you any problems?'

'No! I mean, I don't know, but I'm not on the run or anything. I didn't think to ask you if I could use your address for return of post that's all.'

The one from his sister was brief enough to make Cody swallow at the sick feeling in his throat and wonder at what they had left unsaid:

Dear Cody,
Hi kiddo! I was so pleased to hear from you over the summer. Glad to hear you are getting on well with your adventure. I hope you are enjoying yourself out there still but I can't help but worry what you'll do when the weather turns cold. Charles says that you're a grown man and I must

stop thinking of you like you're a little boy but I can't help it because you'll always be my little baby brother.

Dad is learning how to live as a single man though Sandy and I take it in turns to make sure he has enough meals in the freezer to see him through the week.

Anyway as you have managed to get letters into the mail to me and there is a return address on the envelope, I am assuming you can also get letters written to you. Which is a good thing as mum wants to get in touch with you! I have explained that you're off on a wilderness experience. We have passed your address on to mum and she has said she is going to write you a letter once she is settled in her new home. So I hope the letter you get from mum settles your mind as to why she left and that you are healthy and happy AND that we will get another letter from you soon! Hint, hint...

Lots of love
Lizzie xoxoxo

Cody paused to shake his head at the way Lizzie still drew the dot over the i on her name in the shape of a heart, fondness for his sister flooded him with warmth quickly followed by a sickening adrenaline rush at the thought of what story his mum's letter might contain. What reason could she possibly have for vanishing like that and did he really want to know?

The second letter was from Ellen, and Cody was smiling before he even opened it because she had covered the envelope in doodles featuring smiley faces, trees, wildflowers, woodland animals, a teensy log cabin on the bank of a river, a man chopping wood, a truck, a campfire with fish suspended above it, bunnies with sad faces and a dog with a goofy grin and his tongue dangling from one side of his mouth.

Dear Wildman of Sweet River Camp

I was so pleased to get your letter filled with daily notes of your accomplishments! You are so brave and crazy and fun! Except for the bit about the rabbits, that was icky ☹ I did a doodle each time I read about something new from your day to day activities. Hope you like them!

Anyway, how long are you going to be there? I mean I know you said you had no idea but you must have decided by now. Are you going to wait until fall and Bear is forced to move you on, or are you going to head out sooner? I would like to take you up on your offer to come and visit you but I hate camping! Haha, just kidding, I know you meant in the winter when you have a job and proper roof over your head! AND, my brother says I am not to be thinking about going to stay in a tent with you on my own anyway.

Speaking of my brother I am now an auntie to the cutest little girl that ever lived! My niece Sarah was born just a few days after I got there, talk about good timing. I am not enjoying helping Suzy (my sis-in-law) around the house because it's B-O-R-I-N-G but getting to spend time with Sarah makes it all worthwhile. Sarah is smiling already and is just the happiest baby in the world, everyone says so. I have made some friends and have taken up swimming with them two evenings a week at the outdoor pool. I like that and would enjoy spending more time with them but mostly I am too tired to do anything else because Sarah gets up in the night still and also very early in the mornings. I have the weekends off so I am working in the library making sure the books are on the right shelves and reading to children.

I hope you write to me again soon.

Your friend, Ellen.

Chapter fifteen – The first cold night

In the end, it had been easy for Cody to approach Bear about working in the apple orchard. For one thing, he couldn't stop thinking about what Ellen said about wanting to visit him when he had a proper place to stay. The other deciding factor was that soon as the first cold night hit, he had to accept that although he might have enough food set aside to prevent him from starving, he had done no preparation in the way of getting cold weather clothing or a winter proof dwelling. He wasn't prepared to spend the winter fighting the cold and being unable to spend at least a bit of time with Ellen.

When Cody offered Bear the rest of his food and his help around the farm as a general handy man in exchange for shelter in the barn, Bear had accepted on the provision that Cody agree to live in the house with him and that he allow Bear to pay him a wage.

'It won't be much but a man's got to earn payment for his hard work.'

'I'm grateful for the chance to live somewhere warm and earn my keep. A bit of cash is a lucky bonus.'

The men shook hands, Cody packed his rucksack and they set off for the farmhouse with Jake trailing behind.

'We'll head back and get your supplies in a day or two.'

'Great, wouldn't want them to go to waste!'

'Got a root cellar that'll be perfect for it all. It's where I keep the surplus apples and root vegetables from the garden over winter.'

The men wove their way through the hay field towards the farmhouse in the distance. Jake barked ferociously at a flock of geese as they flew overhead.

'How's he with livestock?'

'I don't rightly know.' Cody confessed.

'We'll find out soon enough, let's hope he's a good'un.'

'What if he's not?'

'Ack, we'll cross that bridge if we come to it.' Bear patted Jake's head as he came back from his futile attempt at geese bothering to walk between the men. Cody glanced down at Jake's cheerful face, and then looked up and away, *I'm not losing Jake,* he thought and lengthened his stride as if to put distance between himself and any possibility of Jake not fitting in at their new home. Bear looked at Cody's tense shoulders; a puzzled expression flickered over his face before he too lengthened his stride so the men once again walked side by side.

'The orchard starts just over there.' Bear gestured at the gentle incline that had come into view.

'I had imagined you lived closer to my camp, though I don't know why now that I think of it, because I never accidently roamed as far as your homestead. Really it should have been obvious that you were a good distance away.' Cody's face added in the 'duh' that he had left out of his final sentence.

'Not too much farther now. I think we should drop your stuff and head back out in the truck straight away while we've still got some momentum, eh?'

'Yeah, okay. We going to get the cached meat and other goods too?' Cody asked, eager to have all his belongings near.

'Makes sense to get it done now as it will all look different round there once the first snow falls. We'll get some firewood on the way back too, I saw some dead fall last time I went out for supplies.'

As they crested the top of the hill, Cody caught his first glimpse of the ranch house. He suddenly understood the phrase, "love at first sight". As he neared the house, several small details clamoured for his attention. The logs that formed the walls of the house were huge and well weathered; this was a house that would withstand almost any of nature's wrath, except perhaps fire. The red corrugated metal roof was a unique twist and one that seemed perfectly matched to the logs in Cody's opinion. The stone steps were wide and welcoming. He longed to walk up them and explore the inside of his new home but lingered at their base while Bear slung his camp gear on top of a stack of wood inside a purpose built lean to. Jake followed Bear and dashed into the woodshed for a curious sniff before dropping and rolling ecstatically on his back.

Bear walked to the red truck in the drive, dropped the flatbed gate and called, 'Up you get Jakey boy, we've got places to go before sundown.'

'C'mon Jake.' Cody thumped the side of his thigh and walked towards the truck. Jake leapt to his feet and raced manically to the truck, jumped up onto the back of the truck and stood there with his head over the side, looking at Cody with what could only be described as a grin on his face.

'Who'sa happy boy then, huh Jake?' Cody reached over and rubbed him briskly behind his ears and then obligingly smoothed his hands over his belly and chest when Jake lay down with his feet up in the air. Cody looked up to see Bear's face split into an impossibly huge grin.

Bear lifted then latched the gate and made his way towards the cab of the truck.

'Stay.' Cody said firmly and followed the words with a stern look. Jake raised his head and looked at him with his ears pricked to attention, then lay back on his side and shut his eyes.

Bear started the truck and Cody made his way into the passenger seat quickly, still unsure of how he should behave around Bear – friend, hired help or somewhere in between. *I'm starving hungry... my belly's trying to eat my backbone...wish Bear had suggested we have something to eat before heading back to camp...guess the trip there and back will be faster this time what with the truck and all...* Cody's stomach grumbled, unconvinced.

Chapter sixteen – Sun warmed wood

The truck was warm as it drifted along the blacktop in the late afternoon sunshine and Cody fell asleep soon after they pulled away from his camp despite the truck's hard bench seat. He woke with a start when Bear turned onto a gravel-covered road. It was full of potholes, which were difficult to avoid even with an experienced navigator manoeuvring the truck along it. Bear had pulled off the main road to use the chainsaw he'd brought along to saw up a few fallen trees. Jake nosed around the fallen trees, careful to avoid the noisier chain sawing area, sneezing and shaking debris off his nose at regular intervals.

'I hate how loud this beast is but am grateful for the ability to make short work of trees this size.'

'Can I help?' Cody offered shyly.

'If you're of a mind to split some logs, there's an axe in the truck bed. Many hands make light work, my ma used to say.' Bear's face grew sombre for a moment before he threw Cody a wink and turned back to his work.

After a few hesitant whacks of the axe on wood, Cody quickly settled into a rhythm and chopped the rounds of tree into wooden quarters and then stored them in the back of the truck snug against the rest of his foodstuffs they had packed into the truck. It was hard unfamiliar work, his shoulders ached and the palms of his hands were blistered at the base of his fingers by the time they'd climbed back into the cab.

'We'll bring in the perishables and leave the wood to be sorted tomorr'er.' Bear said as they pulled up outside the house.

'I'm right grateful to hear that!' Cody grabbed an armload of supplies from the truck bed and aimed his tired body towards the porch light, which was also a lure for a multitude of bumping, bumbling moths. He reached the door and stood aside, realising that the house had drawn him to it with such force that he had mounted the steps without waiting for Bear's lead. Unable to resist the impulse, he shifted his load onto one arm and rested a sore hand on one of the bark free and relatively smooth warm logs through which the door had been cut.

Bear stomped up behind him carrying something he had taken from the freezer situated in the woodshed which bordered the porch. Jake was close on Bear's heels with his tail wagging and nose to the floor and Cody followed, closing the door behind him.

'This will do nicely for a celebratory supper tomorrow,' said Bear satisfaction apparent in his tone of voice.

'What's for supper tonight?' asked Cody, the very thought of food making him salivate. He experienced fleeting astonishment that hunger had superseded his exhaustion.

'My homemade sausages,' said Bear hanging the rabbits on a hook which was suspended from the ceiling in a back room, a blast of cooler air greeted Cody as he moved to look inside. A utility, his mom would have called this room with its stone walls and floor. It served as a store for items that needed a roof and four walls but no insulation.

'Kind of like an above ground version of my meat caches?'

'Close. It's a cold store. I keep all my jars of home preserves in here too and the fruit and veg in the root cellar which I'll show you tomorrow. For now we can leave all of your cache food in here.' Bear handed Cody a towel he pulled from a cupboard in the corridor outside the utility room. 'The bathroom is directly above us. By the time you are done I'll have sorted our meal.' Bear moved to the pot bellied wood stove, swiftly building a crackling fire, seemingly still full of energy.

Cody averted his mind's eye from the sad limpness of the rabbit carcases and headed to the bathroom opting for a cool shallow bath, knowing he'd fall asleep if he indulged in a deeper warmer bath. After washing his body and his hair he felt surprisingly refreshed although a bit woozy. He made his way downstairs towards the wondrous smells coming from the kitchen. They made him feel almost faint with hunger though his desire for food only served to speed him onwards. On the rough-hewn wooden table he saw quilted place mats, cutlery, bread that smelled fresh, a few jars of preserves, sliced pickles and butter. Cody sat without being asked and waited expectantly for his meal, ignoring the pang of loneliness for his mum that the sight of the placemats sent through him. *I'll unpack mum's quilt and lay it across the foot of my bed*, he decided and immediately felt brighter.

'Pour us a cup of that tea please, and get some bread and sweet pickle in you, the rest is almost ready,' ordered Bear.

Cody complied eagerly; making short work of his first slice of the soft loaf topped with butter and sliced sweet dill pickle. Bear brought over a small cast iron skillet and put it on Cody's tiled place mat. In the skillet were chopped potatoes, tomatoes, mushrooms, sausages, which had been all cooked together into a delicious smelling jumble and topped with a couple of fried eggs. Bear sat down with his own skillet and they ate with huge enjoyment while Jake thumped his tail hopefully to the tune of their appreciative noises. The strong tea was the perfect accompaniment to the food. Cody complimented Bear on the sausages, which were coarse in texture, slightly gamey and almost sweet to taste. He had never had anything like it before.

'I'm glad you like them, I'll show you where they come from tomorrow'.

'Show me? I thought you said you'd made them?' Cody was confused now.

'I did, I'll explain tomorrow, I need to get some sleep before this headache of mine turns me into an ogre.'

Bear started clearing the table; scraping the scraps into a bowl he had filled with odds and ends for Jake and set-aside before supper. Now he placed it near the door and gave Jake a pat as he made short work of the contents. Bear filled the empty bowl with water and offered it to Jake again. Cody moved quickly to the sink while Bear was preoccupied and winced as the hot water made contact with his blisters. Cody washed the skillets, cups and cutlery quickly; wanting to help before Bear could offer protest. The mere act of standing while washing the dishes caused waves of exhaustion to pass over Cody. Bear's laugh startled Cody into a state of semi-alertness.

'Your bedroom is at the top of the stairs directly across from the bathroom. Best make your way there now as I am in no state to try and carry you to bed if you fall asleep where you stand.'

'Thanks Bear…for everything I mean. Good night, hope your headache is better in the morning.' Cody made his way upstairs feeling emotional to the point where tears were now welling. He must be more tired than he had realised if Bear's kindness was having this effect on him. He stripped off and crawled under the quilt, asleep before his head landed on the pillows.

Cody woke when the sun came in through his window; he'd been too tired to notice the curtains were open when he went to bed. He nipped out of bed to pull his curtains shut in the hope of having a bit more sleep time. Glancing out of his window Cody gasped, choked on some saliva and began coughing. He sat on his bed until the spasms had passed and then, aware of the chill in the house, he put on the clean clothes Bear had loaned him last night. Buffalos? Cody shook his head in bewilderment at what he'd just seen through his window. He ventured a look out the window again, below was a view of the ranch land to the rear of the house. High fenced meadows swept to the forest edge over two thirds of the view, the orchard stretched away in the other direction and meandering round contentedly within the meadow section were a few horses and an equal number of buffalo.

Cody heard water running then a muted clatter of metal before the smell of the wood fire and coffee wafted up. He hastily brushed his teeth and made his way downstairs, patting Jake who was lying in his new place on the doormat as he passed.

'Morning! How's your headache? Coffee? Can I help? I just saw the Buffalo! And horses! The words tumbled staccato out of Cody's mouth in his excitement.

Bear laughed. 'Good morning! My headache is gone thanks, the coffee is almost ready, and you just discovered where my sausages come from!'

Cody opened his mouth to say something then snapped it shut again. He stared at Bear, eyes wide, lips pressed tightly together and his face white. A look of hurt bewilderment passed over his features. Bear sighed, turned Cody to face the table then put two cups of coffee on it.

'What did you look at me like that for?' He growled clearly pissed off with Cody's reaction to the notion that the relatives of the animals outside were now part of his body.

'You made me eat Buffalo?' Said Cody sickly.

'I didn't make you eat anything city boy. You weren't vegetarian the last time I looked!'

'No I'm just shocked that we ate something so, so...majestic!' said Cody miserably.

Bear drank some coffee thinking through his reply before saying, 'Well I think that is where people go wrong. If you choose to eat meat then I feel you have a moral duty to recognise that some animal has had to die so you can live. Small, medium or majestic, they all died so we could live.'

Cody was quiet; his hands were wrapped round his empty but still warm cup.

Bear continued, 'I decided to develop my own livestock so I knew that they had lived happy, healthy lives before I ate them. I do have a few of what you call Buffalo, although the proper name for them is European Wisent Bison. I also have some chickens, horses, a large garden and the orchard. All of which I expect you to help me with if you stay here. You learned to cope with eating the rabbits and fish you killed in your camp so I'm sure you'll come round to the idea of rearing, killing and eating Bison too.' The sooner the better his tone of voice seemed to imply.

Cody's eyes flew up from his coffee cup to look anxiously at Bear. 'I'm staying Bear, this place is amazing, and I feel so lucky to have met you.' The sincerity in Cody's voice was unmistakeable.

Bear's face relaxed, relief flashing across his features. 'I'm glad you want to stay Cody, I could do with help around this place and I have a feeling we are going to continue getting on fine, city boy. We can't expect to understand each other all the time. Sometimes we'll have to ask each other to explain things, is that a deal? Now let's have some breakfast before we go out to tend to the chicken and horses; normally it gets done before I eat. The Bison sort themselves out but I expect the horses would like some brushing and exercise.'

'Erm, can I pass on the sausages this morning? I'd be happy with some of that bread from last night, not too hungry you see?' Cody lied.

Bear laughed at Cody's poor attempt at deception. 'You are going to have to eat some Bison tonight as we are having steaks but I think porridge and toast will have to be just right for breakfast because Jake finished off the sausages last night.'

Chapter seventeen – The orchard

To the left of the cold store was a door that Cody hadn't noticed last night when they had stored his belongings in there. The door opened onto the world that he had looked down on through his bedroom window.

'Mind your step' Bear ordered.

Bear went through this back door, leading the way. Cody clambered down the wobbly wooden steps one hand clutching onto the back porch edge as he tried to follow in his footsteps and take another look at his surroundings at the same time. Sweeping away from the back of the house was a close up view of the nearest apple trees in the orchard.

Bear followed his line of sight. 'Ayup, they're almost ready for picking. We'll be busier than you can imagine by the end of the month.'

'How'd they get picked?'

'How'd you think, city boy?'

'Uh...I guess if the tree was shaken then the apples would bruise when they hit the ground? So... we climb ladders and pick them?'

'You got it right. Us and a few temporary fruit pickers that is. There's twenty trees in this orchard, would take us far too long to do the job on our own. They'll start arriving in a week or so. They stay in the hunting cabins for the nights they are here and can take away as many apples as they can carry. The rest I sell on in the form of cider to the hunters who enjoy a bit of a drink in the evening after they've spent the day out on the prowl for whichever animal the hunting season is open for.'

'Don't the hunters bring their own drink in?'

'They know that it's not allowed on my land. The last thing I want is a bunch of city boys getting blind drunk on bourbon, going off half cocked in the middle of the night and coming to harm on my land.'

'The cider doesn't get them drunk?'

'Oh it does but it's a different kind of drunk, a milder, more friendly type and I haven't had anyone angry drunk here for many a year. I don't mind the drinking; it's the trouble it can cause even amongst good friends, which I don't like. There's been a few nasty drunken moments out here in the distant past and an angry drunk with a gun is an accident waiting to happen. Restricting what can be brought in seemed a good solution and it helps bring in some extra cash too.'

Their pace slowed as the approached what looked like it could be a barn.

'What do you keep in here? The horses?'

'No the horses are in the stable behind this building. This is where the cider press and barrels are.' Bear lifted the latch on the door and beckoned Cody through.

Cody stepped into black and moved to the left, waiting for his eyes to adjust and for Bear to follow. Bear stepped over the sill and closed the door behind him. Dust motes floated past Cody's deepening vision and he followed them with his eyes, taking in the sight of rows upon row of racked barrels laid on their sides as he did so. The barn smelled of vinegar, dust and mould. It should have been a distinctly unpleasant scent but somehow was anything but.

Bear paused in the middle of the row of barrels and said, 'Are you sweet or dry?'

Cody's face creased as he tried to decipher Bear's question.

'Cider, man! Do you prefer sweet or dry cider?'

'Oh! I don't rightly know. Sweet, I guess.'

Bear twisted the tap on a barrel, releasing a small amount of amber liquid, handing it to Cody and pouring another measure, which he sniffed before taking a mouthful and sucking air into his mouth noisily. Cody watched, then hastily mimicked Bear's actions once Bear looked questioningly at him, noting how the flavour of the liquid changed from a musty scent to a sweet flavour during the sniff to taste process.

'Wow. I didn't think I was going to like it when I smelled it but it tasted totally different to how it smells! Also, it sure tastes different to cider I've had before, it's less sweet and has no fizz.'

'That would be because I make it using a traditional English farmhouse recipe so there is much less overpowering artificial apple flavour that you are probably used to. This sweet cider is known as a 'soft' cider and the dry is called a 'hard' cider.'

'How did you learn how to make it?'

'Oh I found a recipe in the attic here, in a dusty old cookbook, experimented for a few years and finally settled on a way to get the two types of flavours fairly consistently. Learning to work the cider press properly was probably the biggest challenge at first.'

'The press?'

Bear led the way to the far corner of the barn where a large stack of wood and bolts sat glowing wherever sunlight warmed the wood as it filtered through cracks in the walls of the barn.

'We'll be using this soon enough, going hell for leather until we can get all the juice from the harvested apples to start this year's batch of cider.'

'How does it work? Do we just stick the apples between the planks and squish them?'

Bear laughed, 'Almost! We'll pulp the apples first and then layer the pulp in muslin with a board over the top then another muslin filled with apples, another plank and so on. We'll increase the pressure on the layers using these screws and the juice flows through these pipes into our collecting pot. The process is simple as long as you don't put the pressure on too quick and burst the muslin packs.'

'Cool!'

'I hope you still think that when we're finished pressing apples, it gets a bit tedious after a while, especially keeping the rodents and wasps away from the pulp until we're done with it.'

'Urk, that would be a flavour that cider doesn't need.' Cody swallowed sickly and followed Bear as he went out the door near the press.

A metallic clang rang out closely followed by the sound of a horn and tyres receding on the gravel road.

'Ah that'll be the mail!' Bear strode off around the barn and Cody followed casting a glance at the three horses that were tossing their heads, as they took in the presence of this stranger near their stables.

Bear removed several envelopes of varying sizes from the tube shaped mailbox at the end of his drive. He flicked through them where he stood, made a noise in his throat and handed two to Cody.

Cody saw that one was from Ellen and the other envelope was addressed in handwriting that looked like his mother's. He ran his hands over the envelopes, trying to smooth out the creases they had developed during their journey through the postal system, and to sooth his nerves. He tucked his thumb under the flap of the letter that wasn't from Ellen, then thought better of it and shoved them both into his jacket pocket, buttoning it firmly.

Chapter eighteen – Letters

The day spent learning new skills including how to groom the horses after winning them over with treats of leftover apples from last season, left Cody pleasantly drained. The apples were wrinkled, soft and unappealing as far as Cody was concerned, but they had done the trick for the horses and he had groomed them until his arms and back ached. Cody slumped in his chair by the fire after he had finished the supper dishes, *not so different from the after supper routine back home* he thought drowsily, *but I'm a whole lot happier here*. Bear flicked his paper to the next page and Cody's eyes snapped open slowly coming back into focus as he looked at the large rag rug that Jake had made himself comfortable on. He was snoring softly as he slept soothed by the warmth from the woodstove and worn out from his busy day marking his territory and asserting himself as top ranch dog despite the fact that there were no other dogs within miles to compete for the title. The rug that Jake lay on along with the other feminine touches dotted about the house from curtains, to rug, to placemats were all courtesy of Bear's only living relative. His Aunt Honey wasn't well enough to come for visits anymore so Bear made the trip out to see her as often as he could. One evening when he was nearing the end of a cup of coffee laced with a large tot of spiced rum he had told Cody of his parents' fatal car accident.

'It happened on the cusp of me realising that my rebellion against my father's advice to put more effort into my homework so I could get into a good university was doing no one any good. But before I could show him that I was taking my exams and his advice seriously, dad and mum were killed by a careless trucker.' Bear paused, and before Cody could rally his thoughts into a useable order and offer suitable words of condolence, the usually reticent Bear had begun speaking again. 'My aunt Honey stepped into the void and despite grieving for the loss of her brother she worked hard to keep my head on straight, to keep me from destroying myself with regret that I hadn't smartened up soon enough for my father to see.' Bear's voice had cracked at that point and he barked out a bitter laugh. 'I drifted for a while despite her best efforts but she has always said I am the biggest achievement of her life. I do my best to make sure she knows how much I appreciate her. I think they must have broken the mould when they made my Aunt Honey because I've never met another woman like her…'

And, thinking of memorable women, now's a good a time as any to see if this letter is from mum, and what she has to say for herself after all this time. Cody swallowed hard around the lump in his throat as he drew both letters from his pocket, sucked in a deep breath and opened the one from his mum.

My dear son
The girls tell me that you're upset that I left without telling you I was going away for longer than a weekend, and for that I do owe you an apology. I realise that if I had sworn you to secrecy you probably wouldn't have said anything to your

father. I am still not sure that I would have wanted to put you in a position where you had to choose sides between us because your relationship has always been strained.

I have moved myself to a woman only home where we each contribute equally to the living fund. You could call it a commune or a collective I suppose though we just call it *The Retreat*. This place is a sort of shelter for women who have felt they had no choice but to leave everything behind in order to escape their former life. I am sad that I fit that description but am enjoying the quiet predictability of life here and I am selling things I have sewn or quilted at craft fairs to earn my money. I'm feeling more in control of myself and am starting to work out exactly how I feel about a lot of things, but I should think I will be living here for the foreseeable future so I would very much like it if you would write to me at this address:

The Retreat, Meadowsweet Lane, Roanston, Hants, PO2 1JB

I heard that the relationship between you and your father has broken down. I am saddened that you two have had such a serious argument, one that has caused you to flee from home. As I have done the same, I can understand why you chose to leave - perhaps for different reasons or maybe not - this is something that we may discuss in person at a later date. I also need to make my peace with your father – I have written to him but have not had a reply – I expect he is feeling very angry with me though Lizzie and Sandy tell me he seems more sad than mad.

I hope you are not angry with me now that I have had a chance to explain. I felt I had no choice but to run away to a more peaceful place to save my sanity but that doesn't mean I don't love you or your sisters. In fact I miss the three of you more than any words can say.

Love you forever
Mum

Cody let his hand drop to his lap still holding onto the letter and leaned his head back against the chair with his eyes closed and his jaw clenched against the tears that wanted to come. A flood of emotions washed through him; relief that his mum had got in touch with him at last, the urge to crumple her letter into a ball and throw it against the wall, and unexpectedly, a sliver of sympathy for his father. He puzzled over this for a few moments and decided the sympathy was more pity than anything else – his father was a hard man, a disciplinarian above all else, and quick to anger if his rules were not adhered to. But Cody remembered the glimpse he had of his father as a softer man, when he had sat at the table with his wife's wedding ring cradled in his hand, as if this tenderness could somehow be transported to her by osmosis.

Cody's gut curdled as he thought about his mum leaving without telling him despite the fact hat he also understood exactly why she hadn't chosen to take him into her confidence. He closed his eyes, frowning as he tried to make sense of his clashing emotions. Cody decided that he was glad his mum had been brave enough to get herself out of her unhappy marriage at long last. He was relieved to know another man hadn't turned her head, though why that in particular would have bothered him he couldn't define exactly. He felt disappointed that she hadn't trusted him enough to confide in him for the better part of a year, and angry that his sisters has colluded with her in this. Most of all he felt strangely uncomfortable being introduced to the concept of his mum and dad as people with needs and emotions outside of their role as parents. Cody simply didn't know how he felt about anything to do with his parents anymore.

His mum's letter dropped out of his hand, and as Cody leaned over to pick it up, Ellen's letter slid off his lap onto the floor. Cody felt the back of his neck prickle and a thrill ran through him as he remembered the heavy silk of Ellen's voice and the sound of her laughter.

Dear Wildman

Do you have cabin fever yet? Just kidding, it sounds as if you're having a great time learning everything that Bear has to teach you, and I'll bet it feels lovely to have a soft bed to sleep on again. Do you feel like you know what you're doing there yet? Are you going to stay? I might have to change your nickname to Rancher! Those buffalo sound amazing but what I really envy you for is that you get to do so much horse riding. I really miss doing that and it makes me think that I might have been wrong about small town and country living. I have enjoyed my time in the city and having a proper job plus of course all my time with the cutest niece in the whole world, but believe it or not I am starting to miss the quiet of Ganderbrook.

I guess my time in the city has forced me to grow up a bit. Being able to go out and explore all the different city experiences has been fun but everything costs money here, even going to the pool. You can't just go out and have fun for free swimming in the lake or having a picnic in the meadow like you can back home. I would never have thought I would miss those simple pleasures that I grew up with but being away has taught me that the big city isn't as thrilling as I imagined it would be.

Speaking of Ganderbrook, I'm going there for Christmas. Me, my brother, Suzy and Sarah are all going. We'll be driving past Lumen's Gate so I'll be sure to wave as we go past. If you were still at The Randall's you could wave back! I sure would like that actually, to see you, I mean. Maybe we can meet up in the New Year? I don't have to go back to work 'till Jan 5th. Do you want to come here? Or I could take the bus to Lumen's Gate? Whatever, it doesn't matter to me as long as I get to see you in person again. If you still want to do that too.

Hope to hear from you soon!
Ellen

Cody grunted and smiled, reading Ellen's letters was almost as good as hearing her voice again. A surge of guilt about how he hadn't yet followed through on his promise to visit her washed over him. Suddenly the urge to see Ellen was almost unbearable. Cody felt hollowed out by the longing to see her, the emptiness almost unbearable. *Where has that come from all of the sudden?* He wondered. *It's only October, I don't want to wait until Christmas before I see Ellen again. I'll phone her* he decided *write back and phone her. Make plans for us to visit as soon as possible, and again at Christmas time.*

Quickly, before he lost his nerve, Cody said 'Bear? You got any plans for Christmas and New Year?'

Chapter nineteen – Plans

Bear shouted up, 'You just 'bout ready to head back out city boy?'

'Sure am!' Cody pushed away the letter he had been writing his mum, got up from his desk and made his way downstairs. He and Bear had quickly worked out a rota which suited them both and enabled them to get all the ranch work done. They both got up to feed the animals in the morning and then themselves before Bear spent the morning in the office and tending to the barrels in the cider barn while Cody rode through the orchard on horseback followed by Jake so that he was nearby if the fruit pickers needed help or advice. The mornings were glorious, filled with mild autumn sunshine and idle chatter and the occasional less pleasant encounter with a wasp gorged on winter apple pulp and anxious for a fight. The wasps reminded Cody of drunks he had seen at kicking out time, the ones who felt the need to do something with their fists now that they were no longer occupied with feeding beer into their mouths faster than was sensible.

When the pickers broke for lunch so did Cody who joined Bear back at the ranch house where they discussed what had gone on in the morning and what needed doing for the afternoon. Bear spent most afternoons out in the orchard, enjoying the company of the fruit pickers, some of whom he had known for several years now, while Cody did odd jobs around the ranch. On this afternoon's list was the task of cleaning the chimneys of the hunting lodges and repairing a weak spot on the porch of lodge number two.

Cody waved to Bear and headed toward the lodges with the tools he would need, Jake happily keeping him company, though Cody knew he would have to make him lay down a ways away from he was working so that he didn't nose his way into the on-going work at just the wrong moment and end up injured. 'Too nosey for your own good sometimes, eh Jakey?' Jake threw him a look that seemed to be questioning Cody's level of intelligence and Cody laughed out loud. Most things seemed to make him smile or laugh lately it seemed, it was almost as if the sense of wellbeing he felt filled with had to overflow occasionally. *Amazing what a bit of space and time to can to a person's outlook on life* Cody marvelled.

It seemed hard to believe that the winter apple fruit pickers would be gone soon and that the hunters would be there instead. *Which means it will be Halloween before I know it.* Cody thought and felt a slow trickle of excitement at the thought of seeing Ellen again soon.

He had stuck to his resolve to make more effort to stay in touch with Ellen. Cody had been phoning Ellen regularly, a task that much to his surprise he soon grew to enjoy because he seemed to never be short of things to talk about with her. Cody and Ellen had made arrangements to meet up for the Halloween themed hayride in Lumen's Gate after which they planned to stay overnight at The Randall's. Cody had been pleasantly surprised to find out that Howard and Bear knew each other many years ago and were now becoming good friends. They had driven into

Lumen's Gate to visit Howard, Belinda, Darlene and Billy a few times now, which was how the invite to the hayride had come about.

~ ~

'Just think Cody, you and your girl sitting on the highest bale where no one can see if you kiss,' Belinda said drawing out the final word suggestively.

'Gah! Belinda! We're hardly going to be doing any of that. We're pen pals and nothing more!' Cody looked over his shoulder and called for Jake in an attempt to hide the colour that burned his cheeks.

'Oh leave the boy alone,' Howard admonished his sister, 'He won't want to be going on a hayride with a girl he isn't interested in. 'Sides I expect Bear will have plenty for him to be getting on with at the ranch.'

'Just 'cos she isn't my girl doesn't mean I don't want to spend time with her.'

'I don't work him like a slave, and I quite fancy a night in town myself.' Bear said coming to his own defence and to Cody's rescue.

'That's sorted then, we'll expect you both on the night, with or without Cody's friend.' Belinda said.

'We'll set a room by for her though, eh, Cody? Just in case?' Howard winked.

Cody's face flamed again as he said, 'I'll be sure to invite her.' When he mentioned the hayride to Ellen the next time they spoke she had agreed so fast he had wondered why he had felt so worried about inviting her.

'It'll be so much fun Cody!' Ellen said excitement making her voice lilt pleasantly.

Cody could hear her brother say something but couldn't make out Ellen's muffled response until she uncovered the receiver and giggled, 'My brother says he expects us to have separate rooms booked at The Randall's!'

Cody laughed but couldn't help feeling guilty despite the fact that the separate rooms had already been arranged.

~ ~

After convincing himself that time would crawl until he saw Ellen again, the afternoon of the hayride came sooner than Cody had expected. Standing on the side of the road waiting for the coach to arrive Cody felt on high alert, sounds and smells bombarding him, thrills of excitement running up and down his body in direct competition with the chill on his neck from the light breeze. He shrugged his shoulders lifting the collar of his coat higher and stamped his boots trying to pound some warmth back into his feet. Jake dropped a stick at Cody's feet and whined. 'You're going to meet her in a minute Jakey boy!' Jake barked, in excitement Cody thought at first then realised it was all stick love all the way as soon as Jake pawed his leg and huffed pointedly at the stick. Cody turned, walked to the edge of the gravel at the side of the road and threw the stick as hard as he could, shouting encouragement to Jake to find it. He managed to entertain Jake, distract himself and warm up by doing this repeatedly until he heard the coach wheels squeal as it came to a stop on the road behind him.

Suddenly he found he couldn't breath easy because he his heart was pounding so hard. *Get a grip man* he told himself and then Ellen was leaping down the coach steps, whooping with excitement before flinging herself into his arms. Cody was certain there had been no moment as perfect as this one in his whole life. He wrapped his arms tighter around her and buried his face in her hair wishing they could stay that way forever, and from the way Ellen pressed herself against him she seemed to feel the same. The coach driver and Jake had other ideas however.

'Hate to break you lovebirds up but you need to remind this old man which case is yours so I can get on my way.'

Ellen pointed out her case and then squatted down to make a fuss of Jake who was writhing round apparently trying to make his tail and head meet in his paroxysm of joy.

'Thanks Jake…some dog you are, stealing all of Ellen's attention. Man's best friend, huh?' Cody said to the coach driver who laughed as he handed Ellen's case to Cody.

'Looks like he could teach you a few tricks.' The coach driver pointed to Ellen who had her arms wrapped round Jake's neck, eyes closed with a huge smile on her face.

Cody shook his head and whistled softly in admiration. 'Whosa clever boy Jakey?' Jake wagged his tail harder in response, rolling his eyes with delight and, Cody was certain, with an air of smugness over all the attention he was getting from Ellen.

Chapter twenty – Twilight

Cody belched softly, the afternoon snack of coffee and fruit cake settling more comfortably into his belly as he leaned back and propped his feet on the railing of the porch. Closing his eyes he rested his head on the back of the chair, letting his arm slide off the chair until his hand rested on Jake's head. Jake's tail thumped agreeably. The sound of Bear's voice raised in song drifted from the open window of the bathroom. Cody smiled and opened his eyes taking in the view of the snow capped mountains on the horizon for a few moments before he pushed himself up from the comfort of the chair and made his way back in to the kitchen table where his part finished letter to his mother waited for him to add to it.

They rarely spoke on the phone because of the cost of long distance calls but they wrote regularly enough that Cody felt immersed in the his mum's daily life. He found could tell his mum more when he was able to organise his thoughts in writing with plenty of opportunity to reword certain tricky bits like detail about his growing relationship with Ellen. His mother kept Cody up to date with his sisters' news – the latest being that his sister Sandy's husband George had decided to leave the army, and they were now living with Edward. His mum told Cody that Sandy had said it was because Edward needed someone in to care for him and to keep the house in order; the accusation was unmistakable, his mum had said. Cody wondered if the reason Sandy and George had really moved in with his dad had been more to do with the fact that George had been unemployed since he left the army, and this thought plus his outrage at his sister accusing his mum of unkindness towards his father, prompted one his rare phone calls to his mum.

'I'm sure they are all very happy together. Well actually, I'm not! Anyway, I'm well out of it and plan on staying that way. I have no desire to get involved in any way,' Cody huffed.

'It does make me feel sad that you haven't spoken to your father or Sandy since you left.' His mum's voice was mournful and Cody wondered if there was a tinge of guilt there too.

'Lizzie passes on more information than I want and I am sure she does the same about me to Dad and Sandy. Just because we're related doesn't mean we have to like each other. You leaving didn't make me suddenly feel like this.'

When would his mum stop trying to force everyone in the family to get on? Stressed, Cody rubbed his face then began to write to his mum of happier things including a few suggestions for things they could do together when she was out for her visit over the Christmas and New Year festive period. When he had got up his nerve back in early October to ask Bear if this would be okay, Bear had given his stamp of approval straightaway.

'Your mother is welcome here anytime, as is Ellen. In fact, why not invite them both to stay? We've got room to spare.'

Cody thought this was rather remarkable seeing as at that time the hayride, where Bear would first get to meet Ellen, was almost a month away, and Christmas would be the first time he would meet

Cody's mum. 'That's very generous of you Bear; I don't want you to feel obligated to have my mum or Ellen here. What if you don't like them?'

'I don't see why I wouldn't, but if I don't then I just won't say yes so quickly next time!' Bear grumbled out his growl of a laugh and Cody grinned in relief. He couldn't image any reason why his mum, Ellen and Bear wouldn't get on well with each other and he was feeling very excited about spending time with them all.

The lifetime of tension Cody had felt whenever he had to gain approval from another person was less nowadays, and the anxiety over the many 'what if's' of life less overwhelming. He had noticed he was inclined to laugh faster, to smile more, to believe good things were possible.

Cody chewed his pen lid as he wondered if it was time to write to his father, if only to show him that he had grown up and moved on without too much baggage. Cody stood up in response to the adrenaline surge this thought gave him, went through the door onto the porch, walked the few steps to the railing and leaned on it. He was proud of how he had grown in confidence since leaving home and of how much he had learned during that time too. Now he needed to find the confidence to try and explain this to his dad, he wasn't sure why but he had a feeling that this was an important next step for him to take. Cody decided that he would think on the writing of a letter to his dad, and in particular what words he could use to explain how he had redefined the meaning of the rules. He wanted to mark his territory, to show his dad that he was a man now, but also to do it as a more sensible person, without unnecessarily antagonising the old man. He knew now that rebelling just to prove a point to his dad was a battle that had already been pointlessly fought for too many years. Someday, when he had the wording of the letter as perfect as possible in his mind, he would write it down on paper and post it to his father, and the result of that attempt to move forward would be whatever it would be. Cody knew he couldn't control his father's reaction but he had learned that he could modify how he presented himself and maybe this would help heal some of the damage they had both done to their relationship. Maybe they could learn to be polite to each other, even if they never managed to be friendly.

The sound of the water draining from Bear's bath interrupted his reverie, reminding him that there was still work to be done before this day was finished. Not for the first time Cody wondered what his life would have been like growing up on the ranch with Bear as his father. In the short time they had known each other, Bear's generosity, kindness and the way he had learned to keep moving forward despite the hardships he had endured in his own life, had shown Cody the benefits that could be had from looking towards a more positive future. Cody was determined to learned from Bear's example, to accept that what had happened was in the past, to move on and dwell on the pain of his past as little as possible because no good could come from revisiting past emotional injuries.

As Cody clattered down the porch steps hundreds of geese lifted off from the frost covered wildflower stubble in the meadow, filling the air with their raucous migratory flight calls, which soon faded as the birds vanished into the twilight. Whistling, Cody walked with Jake at his heels to tend to the animals' evening feeds, leaving a little more of his childhood unhappiness behind him with each step he took.

THE END

Also by D.J. Kirkby

My Dream of You
Crime of passion or cruel twist of fate?
One summer's day Betty let love carry her a step too far. That exquisite sun dappled afternoon became one of her best memories but also the catalyst for the worst experience of her life. Now elderly, Betty has been running from her past since she was a teenager, and it's about to catch up with her. Will the experience be as awful as she fears or wonderful beyond imagining?

(If you would like to read the first chapter to My Dream of You then you can find it at the end of this book).

Without Alice
Have you ever had a secret? One so important that it feels as if it will tear you in two? Stephen's got one. He's also got a great job, beautiful wife and an adorable son. Outwardly his life seems perfect but it means nothing without Alice.

My Mini Midwife
The pocket companion for your pregnancy with clear answers to confusing questions, and tips to help you make the most of this special time in your life.

Special Deliveries: Life Changing Moments
"*Special Deliveries* is a wonderful collection of stories that pull the reader through a gamut of emotions from start to finish, given all the more impact by the fact the stories are about what really happens behind the closed doors of delivery rooms. From the sadness of the butterfly baby to the joy of a healthy newborn, each one is indeed a very special delivery." Clare Christian, The Book Guru

The Portal Series
Realand, Raffie Island and Queendom are the first three books in The Portal Series - mid grade chapter books written by D.J. Kirkby using the name Dee Kirkby.

"This is great for children to be read to or those who are progressing into reading on their own. It reminded me of childhood books like The Lion, The Witch and The Wardrobe, as well as the wonderful lands that could be found at the top of The Faraway Tree." - Jo D'Arcy - Vine Voice top 1000 reviewer.

About the Author
D.J. Kirkby lives in the South of England in a home otherwise filled with males – husband, boys and

pets – she writes to escape the testosterone. Dee is a registered midwifery lecturer, teaching midwifery two days per week, a registered public health practitioner, working two days per week for her local Public Health Department and the other day per week she uses for author events, Patron of Reading sessions and other writing-related activities.

Find D. J. Kirkby online
Website for adults: djkirkby.co.uk
Website for children: deekirkby.co.uk
Twitter: @djkirkby
Facebook: https://www.facebook.com/DeeJKirkby

Join Dee's quarterly newsletter mailing list to be kept updated about future releases, giveaways and more.

Feel free to get in touch: djkirkby@gmail.com

Now that you have finished reading *The Rules*, please consider writing a review, and posting it on your favourite review site. Reviews are the best way for readers to discover great new books. I would truly appreciate the time it will take you to write and post a review.

Afterword and Acknowledgments
A few years before I finished writing The Rules a reader challenged me to incorporate the words *Bajamawammers* and *Fartknockers* into a future

book. I enjoyed this challenge and would welcome more of this sort. If there is a word you would like me to use in a book please send it to me via the email address above or via the contact page on my website.

Last but not least - Cody's story doesn't end here and a sequel to The Rules will be written (or may already have been written by the time you read this).

Chapter one from My Dream of You

Why Betty Cried

'Mind how you go.' Albie's strong hand threaded with thick veins and dotted with age spots steadied her at the elbow.

The boards of the bridge creaked softly as they moved the few steps to its summit, being careful not to slip on the moss growing in patches where their feet fell. Betty placed her hands on the railing and leaned over to peer at the water, while Albie tried to coax the ducklings and their mother closer from their spot on the other side of the bridge, chuckling as they began to waddle towards him. Betty looked intently at the water, willing her eyes to focus beyond the surface ripples, to show her another glimpse of the fat trout with its iridescent scales. She had seen it breach the water in an attempt to snap up the dragonfly that had come to rest a moment too long on a reed that overhung the bank almost touching the water. The warm spring afternoon was drifting hazily towards evening. I wish I could paint this scene or that I could capture it in a photo, Betty thought.

Albie's words broke through her thoughts. 'Wonder where his damselfly is?'

'Whatever do you mean?' Betty looked sideways at Albie, her eyes in a squint against the glare of the sun.

'I think they travel in pairs. It's the best way to go through life, isn't it?'

Inexplicably, Betty felt a lump form in her throat and she turned to look fully at Albie. Sorrow flashed through her and she was astonished at the strength of her urge to fix the man she loved firmly in her sight. To anchor him to her side forever. To keep him safe.

'You're a handsome beast,' he said fondly, his eyes softening as he reached for her.

Through her half closed eyes, with her heart racing in anticipation of the kiss that would surely accompany their embrace, Betty saw Albie's arms dissolve on contact with her body. Her eyes snapped open to reveal the duck egg blue walls of her room, cloudy without her glasses but assuredly her bedroom, and not the dreamy river's edge capped in blue spring sky that she had been enjoying seconds before. Already knowing what she would find, but unable to stop herself, Betty stretched out her arm to the right. Empty. She knew it would be. Betty moved her left hand around on the bed until she bumped into a warm form that responded with a quiet purr and a stretch before climbing onto Betty's belly. Betty scootched herself up into a semi-sitting position, patting her chest until her cat settled there, waiting to be fussed over. Betty obliged, feeling the tears well in her eyes as she tried to derive enough comfort from this cuddle.

Mornings were always the hardest. Evenings passed in a blur of bath time and reading until she fell to sleep, but mornings, oh they broke her heart. Each and every one of the 240 days since her Albie had gone had damaged her soul a little bit more. Betty pressed her lips into a narrow line, closed her eyes as the despair settled over her.

Sox's purr rattled through her like the gentlest of shakes, a reminder that something besides her misery existed.

'You handsome beast,' she said to Sox who responded by purring louder.

Betty smoothed his fur in rhythm with his purrs from the top of his head, down his back to his tail, over and over until he climbed carefully off the bed then turned to meow pitifully at Betty.

'You want your meaties? Do you?' Sox meowed and Betty could hear him clumsily making his way down the wooden stairs, he always had been much better at climbing up rather than climbing down everything from trees to stairs. I'll take that as a yes, she thought and gingerly got out of bed waiting for the muscles in her back to loosen enough to allow her to stand up straight. Once they had, Betty pulled and tweaked at her duvet until she had it covering her double bed to her satisfaction. She fluffed the four down filled pillows next.

Comforting routines to be adhered to, as there was a life still to be lived.

She washed her face gently with a hot flannel, the unexpected pleasure of this pushed through her misery. As she pulled a brush through her hair, the static crackle the brush emitted as it completed each run through was reassuringly familiar. Dressing gown tied firmly around her waist, she braved the stairs, holding onto the banister and wincing at the sensation similar to grinding glass under her kneecaps as she descended. Getting older is such a pain, but better than the only other option I guess, she thought ruefully. Steadying herself against the wall with one hand, Betty nudged the newspaper with her foot until it was in an upright position up against the wall before bending over to pick it up. She placed it beside the other paper on the table. The other paper for which she cycled every evening to a different store, each night in another part of town.

Blinking agreeably in the shafts of sunlight that bathed her kitchen with warmth, Betty warmed her teapot and left the tea leaves steeping while she sliced a bagel and popped it in the toaster before spooning some revolting smelling tinned cat meat onto a saucer for Sox. He didn't seem to mind the smell and made short work of his breakfast before demanding to be let outside.

'You'd love a cat flap wouldn't you?' Betty said as she patted the breakfast bar chair, smoothing Sox's fur after he had obligingly jumped up. 'But then you'd bring in all manner of rodent, bird and amphibian!' Sox meowed. 'No, disgusting boy,' Betty argued. 'We'll stick to this system, off you go and be sure to meow when you want back in.' Betty opened the door and Sox rushed out. Betty watched him make his way down to the end of the garden in his peculiar manner that made him appear as if he flounced everywhere instead of walking.

Betty slathered her bagel in homemade rhubarb jam which she had set aside from last year's crop. I suppose I should get to the allotment and pick the stalks from this year's growth before they turn to seed, Betty thought before promptly discarding the notion. Too much effort and too little inclination. Pulling the local newspaper towards her, she skimmed through it as she ate her breakfast. Afterwards she moved on to the newspaper from the town where she'd grown up, reading everything from the highlights through to the classifieds.

Nothing.

Betty breathed a sigh of relief. Mind you, she admonished herself it isn't like they would announce it in the paper now would they? Betty watch out we're coming for you!! Yet again Betty imagined what it would sound like when they knocked on the door. She would know they had come for her. She was certain of that. She had heard the police knock on doors countless times in TV shows and their knock always sounded more forceful than that of friendly visitors, and impossible to resist responding to. Betty rubbed her face with her hands. She was tired.

So.

Damn.

Tired.

Of all of this! Of the enormity of this secret, of how it diminished her, and in particular, of having had to carry this burden alone for the past 40-odd years. Mourning her lost chance, she wished she had been brave enough to share this all with Albie. He had been a good man, a kind gentle wise man. He would have known what she should do for the best.